Schubert

Flashing Swords!

#1

FLASHING SWORDS! #1

Edited, with an Introduction
and Notes, by
LIN CARTER

NELSON DOUBLEDAY, Inc.
Garden City, New York

Published by arrangement with
Dell Publishing Co., Inc.
750 Third Avenue
New York, N.Y. 10017

Printed in the United States of America

This first volume of
Flashing Swords
is dedicated, with respect
and affection, to the late
ROBERT E. HOWARD
without whom we would all
probably be writing nothing
but science fiction stories.

Contents

THE INTRODUCTION:

Of Swordsmen and Sorcerers

THIS BOOK contains four Sword & Sorcery novelettes, averaging 15,-000 words each, from some of the most popular writers in this genre. You will find herein a Fafhrd and the Gray Mouser yarn by Fritz Leiber, a "Dying Earth" story by Jack Vance, a Viking Age swashbuckler by Poul Anderson, and the first story in a new series—that of Amalric the Mangod of Thoorana—by Lin Carter.

And best yet: you have never read any of these stories before, because they were all written especially for this anthology and have never been published anywhere until here and now.

IF YOU are a Sword & Sorcery buff, the above ninety-nine words should cause you to emit a shrill yelp of joy; at very least, they should kindle a gloating gleam of anticipation in your eye.

If you are not a Sword & Sorcery buff, well, this book will introduce you to one of the most lively and entertaining schools of fiction popular today, and just might convert you to it.

If you belong to the second category, you might well ask, "What does 'Sword & Sorcery' mean?" A succinct definition follows:

We call a story Sword & Sorcery when it is an action tale, derived from the traditions of the pulp magazine adventure

story, set in a land or age or world of the author's invention—
a milieu in which magic actually works and the gods are real
—and a story, moreover, which pits a stalwart warrior in direct
conflict with the forces of supernatural evil.

While the term, Sword & Sorcery, was coined by Fritz Leiber, himself one of the ablest living practitioners of our craft, the genre itself was founded by a young writer named Robert Ervin Howard. Born in 1906, Howard lived in the town of Cross Plains, Texas, for the better part of his short life (he died at thirty), and produced an amazing quantity of pulp fiction and miscellaneous macabre verse which has, thus far, outlived its creator by thirty-four years.

While Robert E. Howard wrote everything under the sun from pirate sagas to tales of Oriental intrigue, cowboy yarns and ghost stories to sports fiction and murder mysteries, he achieved his highest fame as the creator of Conan of Cimmeria, a wandering barbarian adventurer who roved from one gorgeous walled city to the next across a savage and splendid world of prehistoric magic and magnificence in a shadowy and mythic age which lay between the fall of High Atlantis and the rise of ancient Egypt and Chaldea.

These stories appeared in that most glorious of all the fiction pulps, *Weird Tales*. Although in direct competition with brilliantly gifted and enormously popular fantasy or horror writers like H. P. Lovecraft or Clark Ashton Smith, Henry Kuttner or C. L. Moore, Howard's Conan stories were among the most popular ever printed in that pioneer fantasy magazine. They had a vigor, a drive, a surging pace unusual in fiction of that period (the early 1930's), and they were told with superb gusto and verve and enthusiasm by a born master of the art of tale-telling.

So popular did this exciting new blend of the adventure story, the imaginary world fantasy, and the tale of supernatural horror, become, through Howard's fiction, that when he died in 1936 a number of talented writers stepped forward to fill the gap in the pages of *Weird Tales* left empty by his demise.

Howard, you see, had done something that no one had ever quite done before . . . and this, unless it be a self-defeating experiment, like the prose of James Joyce or the poetry of Ezra Pound, which are too inimitable and too completely personal ever to be successfully imitated, much less continued by other hands . . . this sort of thing, I say, makes other writers eager to try their hand at this new variety of fiction.

Thus, hardly before the sod of Cross Plains, Texas, had covered the burly, two-fisted author who had, in his time, earned more money than anyone else in the town, including the local banker, other writers—like Henry Kuttner, with his Elak of Atlantis stories, and Kuttner's wife, C. L. Moore, with her delightful Jirel of Joiry tales—began contributing to what became in a very short time a whole new genre of pulp fiction.

THAT WAS, as I say, thirty-four years ago. Today, more than a third of a century later, there are at least eight writers who have either earned their chief laurels or done their best work in the popular field of Sword & Sorcery.

Examples of the work of four of them you will find in this book; the other four appear in its second companion volume, *Flashing Swords! #2*. Here is how these twin anthologies came about.

Writers, most of 'em, anyway, are fairly gregarious people and enjoy gathering together with their colleagues to talk business, craftsmanship, and mutual problems. Hence the murder mystery writers belong to a guild called Mystery Writers of America, science fiction writers to a guild called Science Fiction Writers of America, and so on. About three years ago, during the course of a three-way exchange of correspondence between myself, L. Sprague de Camp, and John Jakes, somebody (I think it was me) suggested we Sword & Sorcery writers should also form a guild. Whereas these other, older, larger organizations have scores or hundreds of members, hold annual banquets, bestow yearly awards, and all that sort of thing, we authors of S&S—all eight of us!—would form a genuine do-nothing guild whose only excuse for existing would be to get together once in a while and hoist a few goblets of the grape in memory of absent friends.

Think of it—an author's guild with no crusades, blacklists, burning causes, or prestigious annual awards! A far-flung legion of kindred craftsmen, with no fees, dues, tithes, or weregild. It was a revolutionary concept, and The Swordsmen And Sorcerers' Guild of America, Limited—or "S. A. G. A.," for short—was born on the instant, with three founding members.

As I recall it, de Camp was honored with the title of Supreme Sadist of the Reptile Men of Yag, Jakes received the honorific of Ambassador-Without-Portfolio to the Partly Squamous, Partly Rugous Vegetable Things of the South Polar City of Nugyubb-Glaa, while I basked in the pleasures of the aristocratic title of Purple Druid of the Glibbering Horde of the Slime Pits of Zugthakya.

You may be familiar with the work of one or another of us in certain other fields, such as science fiction or historical novels or whatever; but John Jakes has for years authored the Brak the Barbarian stories, and Sprague has written a number of heroic fantasies laid in his version of Atlantis (a place called Pusâd), while I have thus far produced something like half a million words of swashbuckling fantasy about the adventures of Thongor the Mighty, barbarian warrior king of the Lost Continent of Lemuria.

Anyway, intoxicated with our organizational triumphs, and heady with our success in coining pompous and ridiculous titles for each other, we stopped to consider who else deserved membership in what would always be one of the smallest and most exclusive of all writers' guilds. Fritz Leiber, creator of Fafhrd and the Gray Mouser, of course, came to mind first; and Jack Vance, for his gorgeous "Dying Earth" yarns; and Michael Moorcock, a young English writer who had won an enthusiastic American audience with his spectacular Elric stories. These worthy gents were, in good time, informed of their unanimous election to our ranks.

Somewhat later the membership, then six, was polled and agreed that Poul Anderson belonged with us on the strength of two splendid novels, *The Broken Sword* and *Three Hearts and Three Lions*.

And Andre Norton, too, our only Swordswoman & Sorceress, for her fine "Witch World" series.

So now we are eight.

It was at the World Science Fiction Convention in St. Louis in 1969 that John Jakes or Fritz Leiber or somebody suggested that, with all this raw talent in our ranks, we should pool our octuple abilities and produce an anthology of Sword & Sorcery stories of such stunning brilliance as to rock the work-a-day science fiction world back on its collective haunches. As an added fillip—to say nothing of a key inducement to an amenable publisher—it was decided that the anthology should consist of *all-new* Sword & Sorcery stories, just as Damon Knight's annual *Orbit* consists of all-new science fiction yarns.

A charming editrix, Gail Morrison of Dell Books, liked the idea and requested an original 15,000 worder from each of us, that being, in the opinion of many writers, just about the best length for a good story. The Supreme Sadist of the Reptile Men of Yag gently pointed out that this would make a book of 120,000 words—a tome of somewhat ponderous dimensions. Mrs. Morrison just smiled and said that in that case she would make *two* paperbacks out of it, thus doubling Dell's potential profits; and, in the same breath, she named an emolument so princely that we promptly addressed ourselves to our respective IBM Electrics.

The first volume of the result you hold in your hands.

The fine old art of Sword & Sorcery writing has evolved quite a ways from the era of Robert E. Howard, Conan the Cimmerian, and *Weird Tales*.

Some writers, myself among them, have been content to employ as a setting for our yarns, the mythic epoch which preceded history, as Howard originally did when he set his Conan saga in an imaginary "Hyborian Age" of his own invention.

Others, like my esteemed colleague, Jack Vance, have gone in exactly the other direction, and chose the very distant future for

xiii

their scenery, an earth grown old and gone back again to the primal magic and wizardry it knew in its youth.

Yet others, like Fritz Leiber and John Jakes and Andre Norton, have taken completely imaginary other-worlds as the milieu for their fine stories.

You will find a little of everything, then, in this book and in its companion volume.

You will also find all sorts of stories. Stories with verve and sparkle, wit and polish; stories frankly humorous and stories of sheer, headlong adventure and excitement; stories of action and stories of subtler mood.

But all share one thing in common; they are all tales of swordsmen and sorcerers, in worlds or lands or ages where magic works . . .

LIN CARTER

Hollis, Long Island, New York

Flashing Swords!

#1

Dreamer of dreams, born out of my due time,
Why should I strive to set the crooked straight?
Let it suffice me that my murmuring rhyme
Beats with light wing against the Ivory Gate,
Telling a tale not too importunate
To those who in the sleepy region stay,
Lulled by the singer of an empty day.

William Morris

OF US ALL, Fritz Leiber has been writing Sword & Sorcery the longest. In fact, he has been working within the genre longer than anyone else alive. And he is still busied with the original series he started out with—the heroic and frequently humorous misadventures of an unlikely pair of roguish rapscallions name Fafhrd and the Gray Mouser, which are laid in the colorful and completely improbable world of Nehwon; a series, that, by this late date, has taken on the proportions of an epic, and which, happily, may just go on forever.

Whereas the pioneer authors of the genre, like Kuttner, Moore, Clifford Ball, and Howard himself, appeared for the most part in *Weird Tales,* Fritz published his early Nehwon adventures in *WT*'s only real competitor, John W. Campbell's classic magazine of wacky logic and off-beat fantasy—*Unknown.* The first of all the Fafhrd and Gray Mouser tales, a yarn called "Two Sought Adventure," appeared in the issue of that magazine for August, 1939. That was thirty-one years ago; *Unknown* has followed *Weird Tales* to the limbo of lost periodicals; but the saga of Fafhrd and the Gray Mouser is still rolling along on its wry, delicious, unpredictable way.

Long may it roll!

LEIBER himself is a most imposing gentleman: tall and lean and gaunt, his fine-boned face framed in a spectacular mane of thick grey hair, with a slow, deep voice and thoughtful, humorous, meditative eyes. He looks as if he should always be enveloped in a vast, flapping black cloak, with a giant ruby smouldering at his throat and a slim, rune-etched rapier slapping at his thigh.

Born in 1910, son of the famous Shakespearian actor you may recall from many grand old films like *Anthony Adverse* and the Charles Laughton *Hunchback of Notre Dame,* Fritz now lives and writes in San Francisco. His books have won all kinds of success: *Gather, Darkness!* is by way of being a science fiction classic; *Conjure Wife* has been done both as a movie and a TV drama; *The Big Time* won the Hugo in 1958; *The Wanderer* won the 1964 Hugo as best science fiction novel of the year . . . and there have been other awards too numerous to list.

At long last, Fritz has begun collecting the Fafhrd and Gray Mouser series in bookform, establishing their correct chronology, and penning new tales to bridge the gaps. Five volumes have thus far appeared, and more are in the making. If you, like me, are interested in the sequence of a favorite story-cycle, then let me add that this new story, "The Sadness of the Executioner," belongs *after* what is saga-chronologically the fifth volume of the series, a book called *The Swords of Lankhmar.*

It is thus not only the newest, and the latest, but also—as of right now—the *last* of the Fafhrd and Gray Mouser adventures. But, of course, there will be new tales forthcoming from Fritz Leiber.

Unlike most of his S. A. G. A. colleagues (with the apparent exception of Jack Vance), Fritz does not seem to me in the very least indebted to Robert E. Howard's style. Whereas such S.A.G.A.men as John Jakes and I (in my Lemurian books, anyway) derive closely from Howard, I discern no traces of Hyborian influence on the prose style, story form, or characterization of Fritz Leiber. He himself claims James Branch Cabell and E. R. Eddison as his literary progenitors: this well may be; but I seem to see a trace of Clark Ashton Smith and even Lord Dunsany in his Nehwon tales.

Be this as it may: here is the latest of them all.

2

The Sadness
of the Executioner

by FRITZ LEIBER

THERE was a sky that was always gray.

There was a place that was always far away.

There was a being who was always sad.

Sitting on his dark-cushioned, modest throne in his low, rambling castle in the heart of the Shadowland, Death shook his pale head and pommeled a little his opalescent temples and slightly pursed his lips, which were the color of violet grapes with the silvery bloom still on, above his slender figure armored in chain mail and his black belt, studded with silver skulls tarnished almost as black, from which hung his naked, irresistible sword.

He was a relatively minor death, only the Death of the World of Nehwon, but he had his problems. Tenscore flickering or flaring human lives to have their wicks pinched in the next twenty heartbeats. And although the heartbeats of Death resound like a leaden bell far underground and each has a little of eternity in it, yet they do finally pass. Only nineteen left now. And the Lords of Necessity, who outrank Death, still to be satisfied.

Let's see, thought Death with a vast coolness that yet had a tiny seething in it, one hundred sixty peasants and savages, twenty nomads, ten warriors, two beggars, a whore, a merchant, a priest, an aristocrat, a craftsman, a king, and two heroes. That would keep his books straight.

Within three heartbeats he had chosen one hundred and ninety six of the tenscore and unleased their banes upon them: chiefly invisible, poisonous creatures within their flesh which suddenly gan multiply into resistless hordes, here a dark and bulky blood-clot set loose with feather touch to glide through a vein and block a vital portal, there a long-eroded artery wall tunneled through at last; sometimes slippery slime oozing purposefully onto the next footrest of a climber, sometimes an adder told where to wriggle and when to strike, or a spider where to lurk.

Death, by his own strict code known only to himself, had cheated just a little on the king. For some time in one of the deep-est and darkest corners of his mind he had been fashioning the doom of the current overlord of Lankhmar, chiefest city and land in the World of Nehwon. This overlord was a gentle and tender-hearted scholar, who truly loved only his seventeen cats, yet wished no other being in Nehwon ill, and who was forever making things difficult for Death by pardoning felons, reconciling battling brothers and feuding families, hurrying barges or wains of grain to regions of starvation, rescuing distressed small animals, feeding pigeons, fostering the study of medicine and kindred arts, and most simply of all by always having about him, like finest fountain spray on hottest day, an atmosphere of sweet and wise calm which kept swords in scabbards, brows unknotted, and teeth unclenched. But now, at this very instant, by Death's crooked, dark-alleyed plot-ting hidden almost but not quite from himself, the thin wrists of the benign monarch of Lankhmar were being pricked in innocent play by his favoritest cat's needle-sharp claws, which had by a jeal-ous, thin-nosed nephew of the royal ailurophile been late last night envenomed with the wind-swift poison of the rare emperor snake of tropical Klesh.

Yet on the remaining four and especially the two heroes—Death assured himself a shade guiltily—he would work solely by impro-visation. In no time at all he had a vision of Lithquil, the Mad Duke

4

of Ool Hrusp, watching from high balcony by torchlight three northern berserks wielding saw-edged scimitars joined in mortal combat with four transparent-fleshed, pink-skeletoned ghouls armed with poniards and battle-axes. It was the sort of heavy experiment Lithquil never tired of setting up and witnessing to the slaughterhouse end, and incidentally it was getting rid of the majority of the ten warriors Death had ticketed for destruction.

Death felt a less than momentary qualm recalling how well Lithquil had served him for many years. Even the best of servants must some day be pensioned off and put to grass, and in none of the worlds Death had heard of, certainly not Nehwon, was there a dearth of willing executioners, including passionately devoted, incredibly untiring, and exquisitely fantastic-minded ones. So even as the vision came to Death, he sent his thought at it and the rearmost ghoul looked up with his invisible eyes, so that his pink-broidered black skull-sockets rested upon Lithquil, and before the two guards flanking the Mad Duke could quite swing in their ponderous shields to protect their master, the ghoul's short-handled ax, already poised overshoulder, had flown through the narrowing gap and buried itself in Lithquil's nose and forehead.

Before Lithquil could gin crumple, before any of the watchers around him could nock an arrow to dispatch or menace the assassin, before the naked slavegirl who was the promised but seldom-delivered prize for the surviving gladiator could start to draw breath for a squealing scream, Death's magic gaze was fixed on Horborixen, citadel-city of the King of Kings. But not on the interior of the Great Golden Palace, though Death got a fleeting glimpse of that, but on the inwardness of a dingy workshop where a very old man looked straight up from his rude pallet and truly wished that the cool dawn light, which was glimmering through window- and lower-crack, would never more trouble the cobwebs that made ghostly arches and buttresses overhead.

This ancient, who bore the name of Gorex, was Horborixen's and perhaps all Nehwon's skillfulest worker in precious and military metals and deviser of cunningest engines, but he had lost all

5

zest in his work or any other aspect of life for the last weary twelve-month, in fact ever since his great grand-daughter Eesafem, who was his last surviving kin and most gifted apprentice in his difficult craft, a slim, beauteous, and barely nubile girl with almond eyes sharp as needles, had been summarily abducted by the harem scouts of the King of Kings. His furnace was ice cold, his tools gathered dust, he had given himself up entirely to sorrow.

He was so sad in fact that Death had but to add a drop of his own melancholy humor to the black bile coursing slowly and miserably through the tired veins of Gorex, and the latter painlessly and instantly expired, becoming one with his cobwebs.

So!—the aristocrat and the craftsman were disposed of in no more than two snaps of Death's long, slender, pearly midfinger and thumb, leaving only the two heroes.

Twelve heartbeats to go.

Death most strongly felt that, if only for artistry's sake, heroes should be made to make their exits from the stage of life in the highest melodramatic style, with only one in fifty score let to die of old age and in the bed of sleep for the object of irony. This necessity was incidentally so great that it permitted, he believed as part of his self-set rules, the use of outwardly perceptible and testifiable magic and need not be puttied over with realism, as in the case of more humdrum beings. So now for two whole heartbeats he listened only to the faint simmer of his cool mind, while lightly massaging his temples again with nacreous knuckles. Then his thoughts shot toward one Fafhrd, a largely couth and most romantical barbarian, the soles of whose feet and mind were nonetheless firmly set in fact, particularly when he was either very sober, or very drunk, and toward this one's lifelong comrade, the Gray Mouser, perhaps the cleverest and wittiest thief in all Nehwon and certainly the one with either the bonniest or bitterest self-conceit.

The still less than momentary qualm which Death experienced at this point was far deeper and stronger than that which he had felt in the case of Lithquil. Fafhrd and the Mouser had served him well and in vastly more varied fashion than the Mad Duke, whose eyes had been fixed on death to the point of crossedness, making his particular form of ax-dispatch most appropriate. Yes, the large vagabond Northerner and the small, wry-smiling, eyebrow-arching cutpurse had been most useful pawns in some of Death's finest games.

Yet without exception every pawn must eventually be snapped up and tossed in box in the course of the greatest game, even if it have advanced to the ultimate rank and become king or queen. So Death reminded himself, who knew that even he himself must ultimately die, and so he set to his intuitively creative task relentlessly and swifter than ever arrow or rocket or falling star flew.

After the fleetingest glance southwest toward the vast, dawn-pink city of Lankhmar, to reassure himself that Fafhrd and the Mouser still occupied a rickety penthouse atop an inn which catered to the poorer sort of merchants and faced on Wall Street near the Marsh Gate, Death looked back at the late Lithquil's slaughter pen. In his improvisations he regularly made a practice of using materials closest at hand, as any good artist will.

Lithquil was in mid-crumple. The slavegirl was screaming. The mightiest of the berserks, his big face contorted by a fighting fury that would never fade till sheer exhaustion forced it, had just slashed off the bonily pink, invisibly fleshed head of Lithquil's assassin. And quite unjustly and even idiotically—but most of Death's lesser banes outwardly appear to work in such wise—a halfscore arrows were winging from the gallery toward Lithquil's avenger.

Death magicked and the berserk was no longer there. The ten arrows transfixed empty air, but by that time Death, again following the practice of economy in materials, was peering once more at Horborixen and into a rather large cell lit by high, barred windows in the midst of the harem of the King of Kings. Rather oddly, there was a small furnace in the cell, a quenching bath, two small anvils, several hammers, many other tools for working metals, as well as a small store of precious and workaday metals themselves.

In the center of the cell, examining herself in a burnished silver mirror with almond eyes sharp as needles and now also quite as mad as the berserk's, there stood a deliciously slender girl of no more than sixteen, unclad save for four ornaments of silver filigree. She was, in fact, unclad in extremest degree, since except for her eyelashes, her every last hair had been removed and wherever such hair had been she was now tattooed in fine patterns of green and blue.

For seven moons now Eesafem had suffered solitary confinement for mutilating in a harem fight the faces of the King of Kings' favoritest concubines, twin Ilthmarts. Secretly the King of Kings had not been at all displeased by this event. Truth to tell, the facial mutilations of his special darlings slightly increased their attractiveness to his jaded appetite. Still, harem discipline had to be kept, hence Eesafem's confinement, loss of all hairs—most carefully one at a time—and tattooing.

The King of Kings was a thrifty soul and unlike many monarchs expected all his wives and concubines to perform useful work rather than be forever lolling, bathing, gossiping and brawling. So, it being the work she was uncontestably best trained for and the one most apt to bring profit, Eesafem had been permitted her forge and her metals.

But despite her regular working of these and her consequent production of numerous beauteous and ingenious objects, Eesafem's young mind had become viciously unhinged from her twelve harem moons, seven of those in lonely cell, and from the galling fact that the King of Kings had yet to visit her once for amorous or any other reason, even despite the charming metal gifts she had fashioned for him. Nor had any other man visited her, excepting eunuchs who lectured her on the erotic arts—while she was securely trussed up, else she would have flown at their pudgy faces like a wildcat, and even at that she spat at them whenever able—and gave her detailed and patronizing advice on her metalworking, which she ignored as haughtily as she did their other fluting words.

Instead, her creativity, now fired by insane jealousies as well as racklike aches for freedom, had taken a new and secret turn.

Scanning the silver mirror, she carefully inspected the four ornaments adorning her slender yet wirey-strong figure. They were two breast cups and two shin-greaves, all chiefly of a delicate silver filigree, which set off nicely her green and blue tattooing.

Once her gaze in the mirror wandered overshoulder, past her naked pate with its finely patterned, fantastical skullcap, to a silver cage in which perched a green and blue parrot with eye as icily malevolent as her own—perpetual reminder of her own imprisonment.

The only oddity about the filigree ornaments was that the breast cups, jutting outward over the nipples, ended in short spikes trained straight forward, while the greaves were topped, just at the knee, with vertical ebony lozenges about as big as a man's thumb.

These bits of decor were not very obtrusive, the spikes being stained a greenish blue, as though to match her tattooing.

So Eesafem gazed at herself with a crafty, approving smile. And so Death gazed at her with a more crafty one, and one far more coldly approving than any eunuch's. And so she vanished in a flash from her cell. And before the blue-green parrot could gin squawk his startlement, Death's eyes and ears were elsewhere also.

Only seven heartbeats left.

Now it may be that in the world of Nehwon there are gods of whom even Death does not know and who from time to time take pleasure in putting obstacles in his path. Or it may be that Chance is quite as great a power as Necessity. At any rate, on this particular morning Fafhrd the Northerner, who customarily snoozed till noon, waked with the first dull silvery shaft of dawn and took up his dear weapon Graywand, naked as he, and blearily made his way from his penthouse pallet out onto the roof, where he gan practice all manner of swordstrokes, stamping his feet in his advances and from time to time uttering battleshouts, unmindful of the weary merchants he waked below him into groaning, cursing, or fright-quivering life. He shivered at first from the chill, fishy dawnmist from the Great Salt Marsh, but soon was sweating from his exercise, while his thrusts and parries, perfunctory to begin with, grew lightning-swift and most authoritative.

Except for Fafhrd, it was a quiet morning in Lankhmar. The bells had not yet begun to toll, nor the deep-throated gongs resound for the passage of the city's gentle overlord, nor the news been bruited about of his seventeen cats netted and hustled to the Great Gaol, there in separate cages to await trial.

It also happened that on this same day the Gray Mouser had waked till dawn, which usually found him an hour or so asleep. He curled in penthouse corner on a pile of pillows behind a low table, chin in hand, a woolly gray robe huddled around him. From time to time he wryly sipped sour wine and thought even sourer thoughts, chiefly about the evil and untrustworthy folk he had known during his mazily crooked lifetime. He ignored Fafhrd's exit and shut his ears to his noisy prancings, but the more he wooed sleep, the further she drew away.

The foamy-mouthed, red-eyed berserk materialized in front of Fafhrd just as the latter assumed the guard of low tierce, sword-hand thrust forward, down, and a little to the right, sword slanting upward. He was astounded by the apparition, who untroubled by sanity's strictures instantly aimed at the naked Northerner's neck a great swipe with his saw-edged scimitar, which looked rather like a row of short, broad-bladed daggers forged side to side and freshly dipped in blood—so that it was pure automatism made Fafhrd shift his guard to a well-braced high carte which deflected the berserk's sword so that it whished over Fafhrd's head with something of the sound of a steel rod very swiftly dragged along a fence of steel pickets, as each razor-edged tooth in turn met the Northerner's blade.

Then reason took a hand in the game and before the berserk could begin a back-handed return swipe, Graywand's tip made a neat, swift counter-clockwise circle and flicked upward at the berserk's swordwrist, so that his weapon and hand went flying harmlessly off. Far safer, Fafhrd knew, to disarm—or dishand?—such a frenziedly fell opponent before thrusting him through the heart, something Fafhrd now proceeded to do.

Meantime the Mouser was likewise astounded by the abrupt, entirely non sequitur appearance of Eesafem in the center of the penthouse. It was as if one of his more lurid erotic dreams had suddenly come to solid life. He could only goggle as she took a smiling step toward him, knelt a little, carefully faced her front at him, and then drew her upper arms close to her sides so that the filigree band which supported her breast cups was compressed. Her almond eyes flashed sinister green.

What saved the Mouser then was simply his lifelong antipathy to having anything sharp pointed at him, be it only the tiniest needle —or the playfully menacing spikes on exquisite silver breast cups doubtless enclosing exquisite breasts. He hurled himself to one side just as with simultaneous *zings* small but powerful springs loosed the envenomed spikes as though they were crossbow quarrels and buried them with twin *zaps* in the wall against which he had but now been resting.

He was scrambling to his feet in an instant and hurled himself at the girl. Now reason, or perhaps intuition, told him the significance of her grasping toward the two black lozenges topping her silver greaves. Tackling her, he managed to get to them before her, withdraw the twin, black-handled stilettos, and toss them beyond Fafhrd's tousled pallet.

Thereafter, twining his legs about hers in such fashion that she could not knee him in the groin, and holding her snapping, spitting head in the crook of his left arm and by an ear—after futilely grasping for hair—and finally mastering with his right hand the wrists of her two sharp-nailed, flailing ones, he proceeded by gradual and not unnecessarily brutal steps to ravage her. As she ran out of spit, she quieted. Her breasts proved to be very small, but doubly delicious.

Fafhrd, returning mightily puzzled from the roof, goggled in turn at what he saw. How the devil had the Mouser managed to smuggle in that winsome bit? Oh, well, no business of his. With a courteous

"Pardon me. Pray continue," he shut the door behind him and tackled the problem of disposing of the berserk's corpse. This was readily achieved by heaving him up and dropping him four storeys onto the vast garbage heap that almost blocked Specter Alley. Next Fafhrd picked up the saw-edged scimitar, pried from it the still-clenched hand, and tossed that after. Then frowning down at the encrimsoned weapon, which he intended to keep as a souvenir, he futilely wondered, "Whose blood?"

(Disposing of Eesafem was hardly a problem capable of any such instant, hand-brushing solution. Suffice it that she gradually lost much of her madness and a little of her hatred of humanity, learned to speak Lankhmarese fluently, and ended up quite happily running a tiny smithy of her own on Copper Court behind Silver Street, where she made beautiful jewelry and sold under the counter such oddments as the finest poison-fanged rings in all Nehwon.)

Meanwhile Death, for whom time moves in a somewhat different fashion than for men, recognized that there remained to him only two heartbeats in which to fill his quota. The extremely faint thrill of excitement he had felt at seeing his two chosen heroes foil his brilliant improvisations—and at the thought that there *might* be powers in the universe unknown to him and subtler even than his —was replaced by a wry disgust at the realization that there was no longer time enough left for artistry and for indirection and that he must personally take a hand in the business—something he thoroughly detested, since the deus ex machina had always struck him as fiction's—or life's—feeblest device.

Should he slay Fafhrd and the Mouser direct? No, they had somehow outwitted him, which ought in all justice (if there be any such thing) give them immunity for a space. Besides, it would smack now almost of anger, or even resentment. And after his fashion and despite his occasional and almost unavoidable cheating, Death was a sportsman.

With the faintest yet weariest of sighs, Death magicked himself into the royal guardroom in the Great Golden Palace in Horborixen, where with two almost sightlessly swift, mercifully near-instantaneous thrusts, he let the life out of two most noble and blameless heroes whom he had barely glimpsed there earlier, yet ticketed in his boundless and infallible memory, two brothers sworn to perpetual celibacy and also to the rescue of at least one damsel in distress per moon. And so now they were released from this difficult destiny and Death returned to brood sadly on his low throne in his modest castle in the Shadowland and to await his next mission.

The twentieth heartbeat knelled.

PERHAPS I am inordinately fond of the fiction of Jack Vance; he seems to me one of the most thoroughly entertaining of all modern fantasy or science fiction writers, and the possessor of one of the most brilliant and varied creative talents. He is virtually the only genuine stylist the field has recently produced, unless you wish to consider Ray Bradbury a serious contender in that category, which I, for one, do not.

At any rate, while reading almost anything by Vance, I find myself sort of helplessly in awe of his sparkling surface, his wit, his polish, his dazzling and polychromatic flow of imaginative invention. He tosses off—in the course of a single chapter—more clever and original concepts than most of us can dredge up to add sparkle to a full-length novel. He is a writer to enjoy, to admire, and—if you happen to be a writer, too,—a writer to learn from and to emulate.

Vance is now in his fifties. He was born in San Francisco and currently lives in Oakland—when he is not off traveling the wilds of Ireland or Portugal or Corfu—which is where he was when I asked him for this story, and where he was when he wrote it. A few more biographical data, if you will: an alumnus of the University of California, Vance spent the Second World War in the Merchant Marine, and twice had a ship torpedoed out from under him. Before the War he had sought to become a professional writer, but with about the same bad luck he had later, when trying to avoid Nazi torpedoes. Sam Merwin, editor of *Startling Stories* and *Thrilling Wonder Stories* back in those days, later recalled reading and rejecting a number of "fascinating but, alas, unpurchasable pseudo-

Cabell fantasies" by Vance *circa* 1941; the War was still on when Merwin finally bought a Vance story called "The World Thinker," which I believe was Vance's first sale. Vance, of course, went on to sell twenty or thirty novels and collections of shorter fiction, and to garner a rich harvest of well-deserved Hugoes and Nebulae for such excellent stories as *The Dragon Masters* and *The Last Castle.*

His talents are far too rich and exuberant to be confined to science fiction alone. Under a variant of his name he is the author of several prize mystery novels. And, under his own name, of two simply splendid swordly and sorcerous fictions, *The Dying Earth* (1950) and a sort of sequel, *The Eyes of the Overworld* (1966). It is these two books, of course, that make him S.A.G.A.worthy in our eyes. *The Dying Earth,* in fact, seems in my opinion to be something of a minor masterpiece of 20th Century fantasy: I would rank it beside the better story-cycles of Clark Ashton Smith, those laid in Zothique and the Hyperborea cycle, and with Charles G. Finney's rare little jewel of a book, *The Circus of Dr. Lao.*

While *The Dying Earth* is a cycle of interlocked short stories, which open backwards into each other after the manner of those ivory spheres the Chinese used to carve, *The Eyes of the Overworld* has been described by its author as "a picaresque novel of the twenty-millionth century."

Vance's description of his "Dying Earth" milieu is so succinct that I shall simply quote it: "The time is the remote future. The sun gutters like a candle in the wind. Misanthropic creatures wander the forests: grues, leucomorphs, deodands. The power of the magicians has waned; those still extant spend their energies in plots against each other. In ruins along the coasts of Ascolais and Almery a few languid men and women amuse themselves until that hour when the sun finally glimmers into darkness and the earth grows cold . . ."

Morreion

by JACK VANCE

1

THE archveult Xexamedes, digging gentian roots in Were Wood, became warm with exertion. He doffed his cloak and returned to work, but the glint of blue scales was noticed by Herark the Harbinger and the diabolist Shrue. Approaching by stealth they leapt forth to confront the creature; then, flinging a pair of nooses about the supple neck, they held him where he could do no mischief.

After great effort, a hundred threats and as many lunges, twists and charges on the part of Xexamedes, the magicians dragged him to the castle of Ildefonse, where other magicians of the region gathered in high excitement.

In times past Ildefonse had served the magicians as preceptor, and he now took charge of the proceedings. He first inquired the archveult's name.

"I am Xexamedes, as well you know, old Ildefonse!"

"Yes," said Ildefonse, "I recognize you now, though my last view was your backside, as we sent you fleeting back to Jangk. Do you realize that you have incurred death by returning?"

"Not so, Ildefonse, since I am no longer an archveult of Jangk. I am an immigrant to Earth; I declare myself reverted to the estate of a man. Even my fellows hold me in low esteem."

"Well and good," said Ildefonse. "However, the ban was and is explicit. Where do you now house yourself?" The question was casual, and Xexamedes made an equally bland response.

"I come, I go; I savor the sweet airs of Earth, so different from the chemical vapors of Jangk."

Ildefonse was not to be put off. "What appurtenances did you bring: specifically, how many IOUN stones?"

"Let us talk of other matters," suggested Xexamedes. "I now wish to join your local coterie, and, as a future comrade to all present, I find these nooses humiliating."

The short-tempered Hurtiancz bellowed, "Enough impudence! What of the IOUN stones?"

"I carry a few such trinkets," replied Xexamedes with dignity.

"Where are they?"

Xexamedes addressed himself to Ildefonse. "Before I respond, may I inquire your ultimate intentions?"

Ildefonse pulled at his white beard and raised his eyes to the chandelier. "Your fate will hinge upon many factors. I suggest that you produce the IOUN stones."

"They are hidden under the floorboards of my cottage," said Xexamedes in a sulky voice.

"Which is situated where?"

"At the far edge of Were Wood."

Rhialto the Marvellous leapt to his feet. "All wait here! I will verify the truth of the statement!"

The sorcerer Gilgad held up both arms. "Not so fast! I know the region exactly! I will go!"

Ildefonse spoke in a neutral voice, "I hereby appoint a committee, to consist of Rhialto, Gilgad, Mune the Mage, Hurtiancz, Kilgas, Ao of the Opals, and Barbanikos. This group will go to the cottage and bring back all contraband. The proceedings are adjourned until your return."

18

2

THE ADJUNCTS of Xexamedes were in due course set forth on a sideboard in Ildefonse's great hall, including thirty-two IOUN stones: spheres, ellipsoids, spindles, each approximately the size of a small plum, each displaying inner curtains of pale fire. A net prevented them from drifting off like dream-bubbles.

"We now have a basis for further investigation," said Ildefonse. "Xexamedes, exactly what is the source of these potent adjuncts?"

Xexamedes jerked his tall black plumes in surprise, either real or simulated. He was yet constrained by the two nooses; Haze of Wheary Water held one rope, Barbanikos the other, to ensure that Xexamedes could touch neither. Xexamedes inquired, "What of the indomitable Morreion? Did he not reveal his knowledge?"

Ildefonse frowned in puzzlement. " 'Morreion'? I had almost forgotten the name. . . . What were the circumstances?"

Herark the Harbinger, who knew lore of twenty aeons, stated: "After the archveults were defeated, a contract was made. The archveults were given their lives, and in turn agreed to divulge the source of the IOUN stones. The noble Morreion was ordered forth to learn the secret and was never heard from since."

"He was instructed in all the procedures," declared Xexamedes. "If you wish to learn—seek out Morreion!"

Ildefonse asked, "Why did he not return?"

"I cannot say. Does anyone else wish to learn the source of the stones? I will gladly demonstrate the procedure once again."

For a moment no one spoke. Then Ildefonse suggested, "Gilgad, what of you? Xexamedes has made an interesting proposal."

Gilgad licked his thin brown lips. "First, I wish a verbal description of the process."

"By all means," said Xexamedes. "Allow me to consult a document." He stepped toward the sideboard, drawing Haze and Barbanikos together; then he leaped back. With the slack thus engendered he grasped Barbanikos and exuded a galvanic impulse. Sparks flew from Barbanikos' ears; he jumped into the air and fell down in a faint. Xexamedes snatched the rope from Haze and before anyone could prevent, he fled from the great hall.

"After him!" bawled Ildefonse. "He must not escape!"

The magicians gave chase to the fleet archveult. Across the Scaum hills, past Were Wood ran Xexamedes; like hounds after a fox came the magicians. Xexamedes entered Were Wood and doubled back, but the magicians suspected a trick and were not deceived.

Leaving the forest Xexamedes approached Rhialto's manse and took cover beside the aviary. The bird-women set up an alarm, and old Funk, Rhialto's servitor, hobbled forth to investigate.

Gilgad now spied Xexamedes and exerted his Instantaneous Electric Effort—a tremendous many-pronged dazzle which not only shivered Xexamedes, but destroyed Rhialto's aviary, shattered his antique way-post and sent poor old Funk dancing across the sward on stilts of crackling blue light.

3

A LINDEN LEAF clung to the front door of Rhialto's manse, pinned by a thorn. A prank of the wind, thought Rhialto, and brushed it aside. His new servant Puiras, however, picked it up and, in a hoarse grumbling voice, read:

NOTHING THREATENS MORREION.

"What is this regarding Morreion?" demanded Rhialto. Taking the leaf he inspected the minute silver characters. "A gratuitous reassurance." A second time he discarded the leaf and gave Puiras his final instructions. "At midday prepare a meal for the Minuscules—gruel and tea will suffice. At sunset serve out the thrush paté. Next, I wish you to scour the tile of the great hall. Use no sand, which grinds at the luster of the glaze. Thereafter, clear the south sward of debris; you may use the aeolus, but take care; blow only down the yellow reed; the black reed summons a gale, and we have had devastation enough. Set about the aviary; salvage all useful material. If you find corpses, deal with them appropriately. Is so much clear?"

Puiras, a man spare and loose-jointed, with a bony face and lank black hair, gave a dour nod. "Except for a single matter. When I have accomplished all this, what else?"

Rhialto, drawing on his cloth-of-gold gauntlets, glanced sidewise at his servant. Stupidity? Zeal? Churlish sarcasm? Puiras' visage offered no clue. Rhialto spoke in an even voice. "Upon completion of these tasks, your time is your own. Do not tamper with the magical engines; do not, for your life, consult the portfolios, the librams or the compendiary. In due course, I may instruct you in a few minor dints; until then: be cautious!"

"I will indeed."

Rhialto adjusted his six-tiered black satin hat, donned his cloak with that flourish which had earned him his soubriquet "the Marvellous". "I go to visit Ildefonse. When I pass the outer gate impose the boundary curse; under no circumstances lift it until I signal. Expect me at sunset: sooner, if all goes well."

Making no effort to interpret Puiras' grunt, Rhialto sauntered to the north portal, averting his eyes from the wreckage of his wonderful aviary. Barely had he passed the portal by, when Puiras activated the curse, prompting Rhialto to jump hastily forward. Rhialto adjusted the set of his hat. The ineptitude of Puiras was but one in a series of misfortunes, all attributable to the archveult

Xexamedes. His aviary destroyed, the way-post shattered, old Funk dead! From some source compensation must be derived!

4

ILDEFONSE LIVED in a castle above the River Scaum: a vast and complex structure of a hundred turrets, balconies, elevated pavilions and pleasaunces. During the final ages of the 43rd Aeon, when Ildefonse had served as preceptor, the castle had seethed with activity. Now only a single wing of this monstrous edifice was in use, with the rest abandoned to dust, owls and archaic ghosts.

Ildefonse met Rhialto at the bronze portal. "My dear colleague: splendid as usual! Even on an occasion like that of today! You put me to shame!" Ildefonse stood back the better to admire Rhialto's austerely handsome visage, his fine blue cloak and trousers of rose velvet, his glossy boots. Ildefonse himself, for reasons obscure, presented himself in the guise of a jovial sage, with a bald pate, a lined countenance, pale blue eyes, an irregular white beard: conceivably a natural condition which vanity would not let him discard.

"Come in then," cried Ildefonse. "As always, with your sense of drama, you are last to arrive!"

They proceeded to the great hall. On hand were fourteen sorcerers: Zilifant, Perdustin, Herark the Harbinger, Haze of Wheary Water, Ao of the Opals, Eshmiel, Kilgas, Byzant the Necrope, Gilgad, Vermoulian the Dream-walker, Barbanikos, the diabolist Shrue, Mune the Mage, Hurtiancz. Ildefonse called out: "The last of our cabal has arrived: Rhialto the Marvellous! at whose manse the culminating stroke occurred!"

Rhialto doffed his hat to the group. Some returned the salute;

22

others: Gilgad, Byzant the Necrope, Mune the Mage, Kilgas, merely cast cool glances over their shoulders.

Ildefonse took Rhialto by the arm and led him to the buffet. Rhialto accepted a goblet of wine, which he tested with his amulet. In mock chagrin Ildefonse protested: "The wine is sound; have you yet been poisoned at my board?"

"No. But never have circumstances been as they are today."

Ildefonse made a sign of wonder. "The circumstances are favorable! We have vanquished our enemy; his IOUN stones are under our control!"

"True," said Rhialto. "But remember the damages I have suffered! I claim corresponding benefits, of which my enemies would be pleased to deprive me."

"Tush," scolded Ildefonse. "Let us talk on a more cheerful note. How goes the renewal of your way-post? The Minuscules carve with zest?"

"The work proceeds," Rhialto replied. "Their tastes are by no means coarse. For this single week their steward has required two ounces of honey, a gill of Misericord, a dram and a half of malt spirits, all in addition to biscuit, oil and a daily ration of my best thrush paté."

Ildefonse shook his head in disapproval. "They become ever more splendid, and who must pay the score? You and I. So the world goes." He turned away to refill the goblet of the burly Hurtiancz.

"I have made investigation," said Hurtiancz ponderously, "and I find that Xexamedes had gone among us for years. He seems to have been a renegade, as unwelcome on Jangk as on Earth."

"He may still be the same," Ildefonse pointed out. "Who found his corpse? No one! Haze here declares that electricity to an archveult is like water to a fish."

"This is the case," declared Haze of Wheary Water, a hot-eyed wisp of a man.

"In that event, the damage done to my property becomes more

23

irresponsible than ever!" cried Rhialto. "I demand compensation before any other general adjustments are made."

Hurtiancz frowned. "I fail to comprehend your meaning."

"It is elegantly simple," said Rhialto. "I suffered serious damage; the balance must be restored. I intend to claim the IOUN stones."

"You will find yourself one among many," said Hurtiancz.

Haze of Wheary Water gave a sardonic snort. "Claim as you please."

Mune the Mage came forward. "The archveult is barely dead; must we bicker so quickly?"

Eshmiel asked: "Is he dead after all? Observe this!" He displayed a linden leaf. "I found it on my blue tile kurtivan. It reads: 'NOTHING THREATENS MORREION'."

"I also found such a leaf!" declared Haze.

"And I!" said Hurtiancz.

"How the centuries roll, one past the other!" mused Ildefonse. "Those were the days of glory, when we sent the archveults flitting like a band of giant bats! Poor Morreion! I have often puzzled as to his fate."

Eshmiel frowned down at his leaf. "'NOTHING THREATENS MORREION'—so we are assured. If such is the case, the notice would seem superfluous and over-helpful."

"It is quite clear," Gilgad grumbled. "Morreion went forth to learn the source of the IOUN stones; he did so, and now is threatened by nothing."

"A possible interpretation," said Ildefonse in a pontifical voice. "There is certainly more here than meets the eye."

"It need not trouble us now," said Rhialto. "To the IOUN stones in present custody, however, I now put forward a formal claim, as compensation for the damage I took in the common cause."

"The statement has a specious plausibility," remarked Gilgad. "Essentially, however, each must benefit in proportion to his con-

24

tribution. I do not say this merely because it was my Instantaneous Electric Effort which blasted the archveult."

Ao of the Opals said sharply, "Another casuistic assumption which must be rejected out-of-hand, especially since the providential energy allowed Xexamedes to escape!"

The argument continued an hour. Finally a formula proposed by Ildefonse was put to vote and approved by a count of fifteen to one. The goods formerly owned by the archveult Xexamedes were to be set out for inspection. Each magician would list the items in order of choice; Ildefonse would collate the lists. Where conflict occurred determination must be made by lot. Rhialto, in recognition of his loss, was granted a free selection after Choice 5 had been determined; Gilgad was accorded the same privilege after Choice 10.

Rhialto made a final expostulation: "What value to me is 'Choice 5'? The archveult owned nothing but the stones, a few banal adjuncts, and these roots, herbs and elixirs."

His views carried no weight. Ildefonse distributed sheets of paper; each magician listed the articles he desired; Ildefonse examined each list in turn. "It appears," he said, "that all present declare their first choice to be the IOUN stones."

Everyone glanced toward the stones; they winked and twinkled with pale white fire.

"Such being the case," said Ildefonse, "determination must be made by chance."

He set forth a crockery pot and sixteen ivory disks. "Each will indite his sign upon one of the chips and place it into the pot, in this fashion." Ildefonse marked one of the chips, dropped it into the pot. "When all have done so, I will call in a servant, who will bring forth a single chip."

"A moment!" exclaimed Byzant. "I apprehend mischief; it walks somewhere near."

Ildefonse turned the sensitive Necrope a glance of cold inquiry. "To what mischief do you refer?"

25

"I detect a contradiction, a discord; something strange walks among us; there is someone here who should not be here."

"Someone moves unseen!" cried Mune the Mage. "Ildefonse, guard the stones!"

Ildefonse peered here and there through the shadowy old hall. He made a secret signal and pointed to a far corner: "Ghost! Are you on hand?"

A soft sad whisper said, "I am here."

"Respond: who walks unseen among us?"

"Stagnant eddies of the past. I see faces: the less-than-ghosts, the ghosts of dead ghosts. . . . They glimmer and glimpse, they look and go."

"What of living things?"

"No harsh blood, no pulsing flesh, no strident hearts."

"Guard and watch." Ildefonse returned to Byzant the Necrope. "What now?"

"I feel a strange flavor."

"What do you suggest then?"

Byzant spoke softly, to express the exquisite delicacy of his concepts. "Among all here, I alone am sufficiently responsive to the subtlety of the IOUN stones. They should be placed in my custody."

"Let the drawing proceed!" Hurtiancz called out. "Byzant's plan will never succeed."

"Be warned!" cried Byzant. With a black glance toward Hurtiancz, he moved to the rear of the group.

Ildefonse summoned one of his maidens. "Do not be alarmed. You must reach into the pot, thoroughly stir the chips, and bring forth one, which you will then lay upon the table. Do you understand?"

"Yes, Lord Magician."

"Do as I bid."

The girl went to the pot. She reached forth her hand. . . . At this precise instant Rhialto activated a spell of Temporal Stasis,

26

with which, in anticipation of some such emergency, he had come prepared.

Time stood still, for all but Rhialto. He glanced around the chamber, at the magicians in their frozen attitudes, at the servant girl with one hand over the pot, at Ildefonse staring at the girl's elbow.

Rhialto leisurely sauntered over to the IOUN stones. He could now take possession, but such an act would arouse a tremendous outcry and all would league themselves against him. A less provocative system was in order. He was startled by a soft sound from the corner of the room, when there should be no sound in still air.

"Who moves?" called Rhialto.

"I move," came the soft voice of the ghost.

"Time is at a standstill. You must not move, or speak, or watch, or know."

"Time, no-time—it is all one. I know each instant over and over."

Rhialto shrugged and turned to the urn. He brought out the chips. To his wonder each was indicted: "Ildefonse".

"Aha!" exclaimed Rhialto. "Some crafty rascal selected a previous instant for his mischief! Is it not always the case? At the end of this, he and I will know each other the better!" Rhialto rubbed out Ildefonse's signs and substituted his own. Then he replaced all in the pot.

Resuming his former position, he revoked the spell.

Noise softly filled the room. The girl reached into the pot. She stirred the chips, brought forth one of them which she placed upon the table. Rhialto leaned over the chip, as did Ildefonse. It gave a small jerk. The sign quivered and changed before their eyes.

Ildefonse lifted it and in a puzzled voice read: "Gilgad!"

Rhialto glanced furiously at Gilgad, who gave back a bland stare. Gilgad had also halted time, but Gilgad had waited until the chip was actually upon the table.

Ildefonse said in a muffled voice, "That is all. You may go." The girl departed. Ildefonse poured the chips on the table. They

27

were correctly indited; each bore the sign or the signature of one of the magicians present. Ildefonse pulled at his white beard. He said, "It seems that Gilgad has availed himself of the IOUN stones."

Gilgad strode to the table. He emitted a terrible cry. "The stones! What has been done to them?" He held up the net, which now sagged under the weight of its contents. The brooding translucence was gone; the objects in the net shone with a vulgar vitreous glitter. Gilgad took one and dashed it to the floor, where it shattered into splinters. "These are not the IOUN stones! Knavery is afoot!"

"Indeed!" declared Ildefonse. "So much is clear."

"I demand my stones!" raved Gilgad. "Give them to me at once or I loose a spell of anguish against all present!"

"One moment," growled Hurtiancz. "Delay your spell. Ildefonse, bring forth your ghost; learn what transpired."

Ildefonse gave his beard a dubious tug, then raised his finger toward the far corner. "Ghost! Are you at hand?"

"I am."

"What occurred while we drew chips from the pot?"

"There was motion. Some moved, some stayed. When the chip at last was laid on the table, a strange shape passed into the room. It took the stones and was gone."

"What manner of strange shape?"

"It wore a skin of blue scales; black plumes rose from its head: still it carried a soul of man."

"Archveult!" muttered Hurtiancz. "I suspect Xexamedes!"

Gilgad cried, "So then, what of my stones, my wonderful stones? How will I regain my property? Must I always be stripped of my valued possessions?"

"Cease your keening!" snapped the diabolist Shrue. "The remaining items must be distributed. Ildefonse, be so good as to consult the lists."

Ildefonse took up the papers. "Since Gilgad won the first draw, his list will now be withdrawn. For second choice—"

28

He was interrupted by Gilgad's furious complaint. "I protest this intolerable injustice! I won nothing but a handful of glass gewgaws!"

Ildefonse shrugged. "It is the robber archveult to whom you must complain, especially when the drawing was attended by certain temporal irregularities, to which I need make no further reference."

Gilgad raised his arms in the air; his saturnine face knotted to the surge and countersurge of his passions. His colleagues watched with dispassionate faces. "Proceed, Ildefonse," said Vermoulian the Dream-walker.

Ildefonse spread out the papers. "It appears that among the group only Rhialto, for second choice, has selected this curiously-shaped device, which appears to be one of Houlart's Preterite Recordiums. I therefore make this award and place Rhialto's list with Gilgad's. Perdustin, Barbanikos, Ao of the Opals, and I myself have evinced a desire for this Casque of Sixty Directions, and we must therefore undertake a trial by lot. . . . The jar, four chips—"

"On this occasion," said Perdustin, "let the maid be brought here now. She will put her hand over the mouth of the pot; we will insert the chips between her fingers; thus we ensure against a disruption of the laws of chance."

Ildefonse pulled at his white whiskers, but Perdustin had his way. In this fashion all succeeding lots were drawn. Presently it became Rhialto's turn to make a free choice.

"Well then, Rhialto," said Ildefonse. "What do you select?"

Rhialto's resentment boiled up in his throat. "As restitution for my seventeen exquisite bird-women, my ten-thousand-year-old way-post, I am supposed to be gratified with this packet of Stupefying Dust?"

Ildefonse spoke soothingly. "Human interactions, stimulated as they are by disequilibrium, never achieve balance. In even the most favorable transaction, one party—whether he realizes it or not—must always come out the worse."

"The proposition is not unknown to me," said Rhialto in a more reasonable voice. "However—"

Zilifant uttered a sudden startled cry. "Look!" He pointed to the great mantelpiece; here, camouflaged by the carving, hung a linden leaf. With trembling fingers Ildefonse plucked it down. Silver characters read:

MORREION LIVES A DREAM.
NOTHING IS IMMINENT!

"Ever more confusing," muttered Hurtiancz. "Xexamedes persists in reassuring us that all is well with Morreion: an enigmatic exercise!"

"It must be remembered," the ever cautious Haze pointed out, "that Xexamedes, a renegade, is enemy to all."

Herark the Harbinger, held up a black-enameled fore-finger. "My habit is to make each problem declare its obverse. The first message, 'NOTHING THREATENS MORREION', becomes 'SOMETHING DOES NOT THREATEN MORREION'; and again: 'NOTHING DOES THREATEN MORREION'."

"Verbiage, prolixity!" grumbled the practical Hurtiancz.

"Not so fast!" said Zilifant. "Herark is notoriously profound! 'NOTHING' might be intended as a delicate reference to death: a niceness of phrase, so to speak."

"Was Xexamedes famous for his exquisite good taste?" asked Hurtiancz with heavy sarcasm. "I think not. Like myself, when he meant 'death' he said 'death'."

"My point exactly!" cried Herark. "I ask myself: what is this 'Nothing', which threatens Morreion? Shrue, what or where is 'Nothing'?"

Shrue hunched his thin shoulders. "It is not to be found among the demon-lands."

"Vermoulian, in your peregrine palace you have traveled far: where or what is 'Nothing'?"

30

Vermoulian the Dream-walker declared his perplexity. "I have never discovered such a place."

"Mune the Mage: what or where is Nothing?"

"Somewhere," reflected Mune the Mage, "I have seen a reference to 'Nothing', but I cannot recall the connection."

"The key word is 'reference'," stated Herark. "Ildefonse, be so good as to consult the Great Gloss."

Ildefonse selected a volume from a shelf, threw back the broad covers. " 'Nothing'. Various topical references. . . . A metaphysical description. . . . A place? *'Nothing: the non-region beyond the end of the cosmos.' "*

Hurtiancz suggested, "For good measure, why not consult the entry 'Morreion'?"

Somewhat reluctantly Ildefonse found the reference. He read: " *'Morreion: A legendary hero of the 43rd Aeon, who vanquished the archveults and drove them aghast to Jangk. Thereupon they took him as far as the mind can reach, to the shining fields where they win their IOUN stones. His erstwhile comrades, who had vowed their protection, put him out of mind, and thereafter nought can be said.'* A biased and inaccurate statement, but interesting nonetheless."

Vermoulian the Dream-walker rose to his feet. "I have been planning an extended journey in my palace; this being the case I will take it upon myself to seek Morreion."

Gilgad gave a croak of fury and dismay. "You think to explore the 'shining fields'! It is I who has earned that right, not you!"

Vermoulian, a large man, sleek as a seal, with a pallid inscrutable face, declared: "My exclusive purpose is to rescue the hero Morreion; the IOUN stones to me are no more than an idle afterthought."

Ildefonse spoke: "Well said! But you will work more efficaciously with a very few trusted colleagues, perhaps myself alone."

"Precisely correct!" asserted Rhialto. "But a third person of proved resource is necessary in the event of danger. I also will share the hardships; otherwise I would think ill of myself."

Hurtiancz spoke with truculent fervor. "I never have been one to hold back! You may rely upon me."

"The presence of a Necrope is indispensable," stated Byzant. "I must therefore accompany the group."

Vermoulian asserted his preference for traveling alone, but no one would listen. Vermoulian at last capitulated, with a peevish droop to his usually complacent countenance. "I leave at once. If any are not at the palace within the hour I will understand that they have changed their minds."

"Come, come!" chided Ildefonse. "I need three and a half hours simply to instruct my staff! We require more time."

"The message declared: 'NOTHING IS IMMINENT'," said Vermoulian. "Haste is of the essence!"

"We must take the word in its context," said Ildefonse. "Morreion has known his present condition several aeons; the word 'imminent' may well designate a period of five hundred years."

With poor grace Vermoulian agreed to delay his departure until the following morning.

5

THE ANCIENT SUN sank behind the Scaum hills; thin black clouds hung across the maroon afterlight. Rhialto arrived at the outer portal to his domain. He gave a signal and waited confidently for Puiras to lift the boundary curse.

The manse showed no responsive sign.

Rhialto made another signal, stamping impatiently. From the nearby forest of sprawling kang trees came the moaning of a grue, arousing the hairs at the back of Rhialto's neck. He flashed his finger-beams once more: where was Puiras? The white jade tiles of the roof loomed pale through the twilight. He saw no lights.

From the forest the grue moaned again and in a plaintive voice called out for solace. Rhialto tested the boundary with a branch, to discover no curse, no protection whatever.

Flinging down the branch, he strode to the manse. All seemed to be in order, though Puiras was nowhere to be found. If he had scoured the hall, the effort was not noticeable. Shaking his head in deprecation, Rhialto went to examine the way-post, which was being repaired by his Minuscules. The superintendent flew up on a mosquito to render his report; it seemed that Puiras had neglected to set out the evening victuals. Rhialto did so now and added half an ounce of jellied eel at his own expense.

With a dram of Blue Ruin at his elbow, Rhialto examined the convoluted tubes of bronze which he had brought from the castle of Ildefonse: the so-called 'Preterite Recordium'. He tried to trace the course of the tubes but they wound in and out in a most confusing fashion. He gingerly pressed one of the valves, to evoke a sibilant whispering from the horn. He touched another, and now he heard a far-off guttural song. The sound came not from the horn, but from the pathway, and a moment later Puiras lurched through the door. He turned a vacuous leer toward Rhialto and staggered off toward his quarters.

Rhialto called sharply: "Puiras!"

The servitor lurched about. "What then?"

"You have taken too much to drink; in consequence you are drunk."

Puiras ventured a knowing smirk. "Your perspicacity is keen, your language is exact. I take no exception to either remark."

Rhialto said, "I have no place for an irresponsible or bibulous servant. You are hereby discharged."

"No, you don't!" cried Puiras in a coarse voice, and emphasized the statement with a belch. "They told me I'd have a good post if I stole no more than old Funk and praised your noble airs. Well then! Tonight I stole only moderately, and from me the lack of insult is high praise. So there's the good post and what's a good post without a walk to the village?"

33

"Puiras, you are dangerously intoxicated," said Rhialto. "What a disgusting sight you are indeed!"

"No compliments!" roared Puiras. "We can't all be fine magicians with fancy clothes at the snap of a finger."

In outrage Rhialto rose to his feet. "Enough! Be off to your quarters before I inflict a torment upon you!"

"That's where I was going when you called me back," replied Puiras sulkily.

Rhialto conceived a further rejoinder to be beneath his dignity; Puiras stumbled away, muttering under his breath.

6

AT REST upon the ground Vermoulian's wonderful peregrine palace, together with its loggias, formal gardens and entrance pavilion, occupied an octagonal site some three acres in extent. The plan of the palace proper was that of a four-pointed star, with a crystal spire at each apex and a spire, somewhat taller, at the center, in which Vermoulian maintained his private chambers. A marble balustrade enclosed the forward pavilion. At the center a fountain raised a hundred jets of water; to either side grew lime trees with silver blossoms and silver fruit. The quadrangles to the right and left were laid out as formal gardens; the area at the rear was planted with herbs and salads for the palace kitchen.

Vermoulian's guests occupied suites in the wings; under the central spire were the various salons, the morning and afternoon rooms, the library, the music chamber, the formal dining room and the lounge.

An hour after sunrise the magicians began to arrive, with Gilgad first on the scene and Ildefonse the last. Vermoulian, his nonchalance restored, greeted each magician with carefully measured affability. After inspecting their suites the magicians gathered in the grand salon. Vermoulian addressed the group. "It is my great pleasure to entertain so distinguished a company! Our goal: the rescue of the hero Morreion! All present are keen and dedicated —but do all understand that we must wander far regions?" Vermoulian turned his placid gaze from face to face. "Are all prepared for tedium, discomfort and danger? Such may well eventuate, and if any have doubts or if any pursue subsidiary goals, such as a search for IOUN stones, now is the time for these persons to return to their respective manses, castles, caves, and eyries. Are any so inclined? No? We depart."

Vermoulian bowed to his now uneasy guests. He mounted to the control belvedere where he cast a spell of buoyancy upon the palace; it rose to drift on the morning breeze like a pinnacled cloud. Vermoulian consulted his Celestial Almanac and made note of certain symbols; these he inscribed upon the carnelian mandate wheel, which he set into rotation; the signs were spun off into the interflux, to elucidate a route across the universe. Vermoulian fired a taper and held it to the speed-incense; the palace departed; ancient Earth and the waning sun were left behind.

Beside the marble balustrade stood Rhialto. Ildefonse came to join him; the two watched Earth dwindle to a rosy pink crescent. Ildefonse spoke in a melancholy voice: "When one undertakes a journey of this sort, where the event is unknown, long thoughts come of their own accord. I trust that you left your affairs in order?"

"My household is not yet settled," said Rhialto. "Puiras has proved unsatisfactory; when drunk he sings and performs grotesque capers; when sober he is as surly as a leech on a corpse. This morning I demoted him to Minuscule."

Ildefonse nodded absently. "I am troubled by what I fear to be cross-purposes among our colleagues, worthy fellows though they may be."

"You refer to the 'shining fields' of IOUN stones?" Rhialto put forward delicately.

"I do. As Vermoulian categorically declared, we fare forth to the rescue of Morreion. The IOUN stones can only prove a distraction. Even if a supply were discovered, I suspect that the interests of all might best be served by a highly selective distribution, the venal Gilgad's complaints notwithstanding."

"There is much to be said for this point of view," Rhialto admitted. "It is just as well to have a prior understanding upon a matter so inherently controversial. Vermoulian of course must be allotted a share."

"This goes without saying."

At this moment Vermoulian descended to the pavilion where he was approached by Mune the Mage, Hurtiancz and others. Mune raised a question regarding their destination. "The question of ultimates becomes important. How, Vermoulian, can you know that this precise direction will take us to Morreion?"

"A question well put," said Vermoulian. "To respond, I must cite an intrinsic condition of the universe. We set forth in any direction which seems convenient; each leads to the same place: the end of the universe."

"Interesting!" declared Zilifant. "In this case, we must inevitably find Morreion: an encouraging prospect!"

Gilgad was not completely satisfied. "What of the 'shining fields' in the reference? Where are these located?"

"A matter of secondary or even tertiary concern," Ildefonse reminded him. "We must think only of the hero Morreion."

"Your solicitude is late by several aeons," said Gilgad waspishly. "Morreion may well have grown impatient."

"Other circumstances intervened," said Ildefonse with a frown of annoyance. "Morreion will certainly understand the situation."

Zilifant remarked, "The conduct of Xexamedes becomes ever more puzzling! As a renegade archveult, he has no ostensible reason to oblige either Morreion, the archveults, or ourselves."

"The mystery in due course will be resolved," said Herark the Harbinger.

36

7

So WENT the voyage. The palace drifted through the stars, under and over clouds of flaming gas, across gulfs of deep black space. The magicians meditated in the pergolas, exchanged opinions in the salons over goblets of liquor, lounged upon the marble benches of the pavilion, leaned on the balustrade to look down at the galaxies passing below. Breakfasts were served in the individual suites, luncheons were usually set forth al fresco on the pavilion, the dinners were sumptuous and formal and extended far into the night. To enliven these evenings Vermoulian called forth the most charming, witty and beautiful women of all the past eras, in their quaint and splendid costumes. They found the peregrine palace no less remarkable than the fact of their own presence aboard. Some thought themselves dreaming; others conjectured their own deaths; a few of the more sophisticated made the correct presumption. To facilitate social intercourse Vermoulian gave them command of contemporary language, and the evenings frequently became merry affairs. Rhialto became enamoured of a certain Mersei from the land of Mith, long since foundered under the waters of the Shan Ocean. Mersei's charm resided in her slight body, her grave pale face behind which thoughts could be felt but not seen. Rhialto plied her with all gallantry, but she failed to respond, merely looking at him in disinterested silence, until Rhialto wondered if she were slack-witted, or possibly more subtle than himself. Either case made him uncomfortable, and he was not sorry when Vermoulian returned this particular group to oblivion.

Through clouds and constellations they moved, past bursting galaxies and meandering star-streams; through a region where the stars showed a peculiar soft violet and hung in clouds of pale green gas; across a desolation where nothing whatever was seen save a few far luminous clouds. Then presently they came to a new region, where blazing white giants seemed to control whirlpools of pink, blue and white gas, and the magicians lined the balustrade looking out at the spectacle.

At last the stars thinned, the great star-streams were lost in the distance. Space seemed darker and heavier, and finally there came a time when all the stars were behind and nothing lay ahead but darkness. Vermoulian made a grave announcement. "We are now close to the end of the universe! We must go with care. 'Nothing' lies ahead."

"Where then is Morreion?" demanded Hurtiancz. "Surely he is not to be found wandering vacant space."

"Space is not yet vacant," stated Vermoulian. "Here, there and roundabout, are dead stars and wandering star-hulks; in a sense, we traverse the refuse-heap of the universe, where the dead stars come to await a final destiny; and notice, yonder, far ahead: a single star, the last in the universe. We must approach with caution; beyond lies 'Nothing'."

" 'Nothing' is not yet visible," remarked Ao of the Opals.

"Look more closely!" said Vermoulian. "Do you see that far dark wall? That is 'Nothing'."

"Again," said Perdustin, "the question arises: where is Morreion? Back at Ildefonse's castle, when we formed conjectures, the end of the universe seemed a definite spot. Now that we are here, we find a considerable latitude of choice."

Gilgad muttered, half to himself: "The expedition is a farce. I see no 'fields', shining or otherwise."

Vermoulian said, "The solitary star would seem an initial object of investigation. We approach at a rash pace; I must slake the the speed-incense."

The magicians stood by the balustrade watching as the far star waxed in brightness. Vermoulian called down from the belvedere to announce a lone planet in orbit around the sun.

"A possibility thereby exists," stated Mune the Mage, "that on this very planet we may find Morreion."

8

THE PALACE moved down to the solitary star and the lone planet became a disk the color of moth-wing. Beyond, clearly visible in the wan sunlight, stood the ominous black wall. Hurtiancz said, "Xexamedes' warning now becomes clear—assuming, of course, that Morreion inhabits this drab and isolated place."

The world gradually expanded, to show a landscape dreary and worn. A few decayed hills rose from the plains; as many ponds gleamed sullenly in the sunlight. The only other features of note were the ruins of once extensive cities; a very few buildings had defied the ravages of time sufficiently to display a squat and distorted architecture.

The palace settled close above one of the ruins; a band of small weasel-like rodents bounded away into the scrub; no other sign of life was evident. The palace continued west around the planet. Vermoulian presently called down from the belvedere: "Notice the cairn; it marks an ancient thoroughfare."

Other cairns at three-mile intervals appeared, mounds of carefully fitted stones six feet high; they marked a way around the planet.

At the next tumble of ruins Vermoulian, observing a level area, allowed the palace to settle so that the ancient city and its cluster of surviving structures might be explored.

The magicians set off in various directions, the better to pursue their investigations. Gilgad went toward the desolate plaza, Perdustin and Zilifant to the civic amphitheatre, Hurtiancz into a nearby tumble of sandstone blocks. Ildefonse, Rhialto, Mune

39

the Mage and Herark the Harbinger wandered at random, until a raucous chanting brought them up short.

"Peculiar!" exclaimed Herark. "It sounds like the voice of Hurtiancz, the most dignified of men!"

The group entered a cranny through the ruins, which opened into a large chamber, protected from sifting sand by massive blocks of rock. Light filtered through various chinks and apertures; down the middle ran a line of six long slabs. At the far end sat Hurtiancz, watching the entry of the magicians with an imperturbable gaze. On the slab in front of him stood a globe of dark brown glass, or glazed stone. A rack behind him held other similar bottles.

"It appears," said Ildefonse, "that Hurtiancz has stumbled upon the site of the ancient tavern."

"Hurtiancz!" Rhialto called out. "We heard your song and came to investigate. What have you discovered?"

Hurtiancz hawked and spat on the ground. "Hurtiancz!" cried Rhialto. "Do you hear me? Or have you taken too much of this ancient tipple to be sensible?"

Hurtiancz replied in a clear voice, "In one sense I have taken too much; in another, not enough."

Mune the Mage picked up the brown glass bottle and smelled the contents. "Astringent, tart, herbal." He tasted the liquid. "It is quite refreshing."

Ildefonse and Herark the Harbinger each took a brown glass globe from the rack and broke open the bung; they were joined by Rhialto and Mune the Mage.

Ildefonse, as he drank, became garrulous, and presently he fell to speculating in regard to the ancient city. ". . . Just as from one bone the skilled palaeontologist deduces an entire skeleton, so from a single artifact, the qualified scholar reconstructs every aspect of the responsible race. As I taste this liquor, as I examine this bottle, I ask myself: what do the dimensions, textures, colors and flavors betoken? No intelligent act is without symbolic significance."

Hurtiancz, upon taking drink, tended to become gruff and surly. Now he stated in an uncompromising voice: "The subject is of small import."

Ildefonse was not to be deterred. "Here the pragmatic Hurtiancz and I, the man of many parts, are at variance. I was about to carry my argument a step farther, and in fact I will do so, stimulated as I am by this elixir of a vanished race. I therefore suggest that, in the style of the previous examples, a natural scientist, examining a single atom, might well be able to asseverate the structure and history of the entire universe!"

"Bah!" muttered Hurtiancz. "By the same token, a sensible man needs listen to but a single word in order to recognize the whole for egregious nonsense."

Ildefonse, absorbed in his theories, paid no heed. Herark took occasion to state that in his opinion, not one, but at least two, even better, three of any class of objects was essential to understanding. "I cite the discipline of mathematics, where a series may not be determined by less than three terms."

"I willingly grant the scientist his three atoms," said Ildefonse, "though in the strictest sense, two of these are supererogatory."

Rhialto, rising from his slab, went to look into a dirt-choked aperture, to discover a passage descending by broad steps into the ground. He caused an illumination to proceed before him and descended the steps. The passage turned once, turned twice, then opened into a large chamber paved with brown stone. The walls held a number of niches, six feet long, two feet high, three feet deep; peering into one of these Rhialto discovered a skeleton of most curious structure, so fragile that the impact of Rhialto's gaze caused it to collapse into dust.

Rhialto rubbed his chin. He looked into a second niche to discover a similar skeleton. He backed away, and stood musing a moment or two. Then he returned up the steps, the drone of Ildefonse's voice growing progressively louder: "—in the same manner to the question: why does the universe end here and not a mile farther? Of all questions, *why?* is the least pertinent. It begs the question; it assumes the larger part of its own response: to wit, that a sensible response exists." Ildefonse paused to refresh himself, and Rhialto took occasion to relate his discoveries in the chamber below.

"It appears to be a crypt," said Rhialto. "The walls are lined with niches, and each contains the veriest wraith of a dead corpse."

"Indeed, indeed!" muttered Hurtiancz. He lifted the brown glass bottle and at once put it down.

"Perhaps we are mistaken in assuming this place a tavern," Rhialto continued. "The liquid in the bottles, rather than tipple, I believe to be embalming fluid."

Ildefonse was not so easily diverted. "I now propound the basic and elemental verity: what is IS. Here you have heard the basic proposition of magic. What magician asks *Why?* He asks *How?;* *Why?* leads to stultification; each response generates at least one other question, in this fashion:

"Question? Why does Rhialto wear a black hat with gold tassels and a scarlet plume?

"Answer: Because he hopes to improve his semblance.

"Question: Why does he want to improve his semblance?

"Answer: Because he craves the admiration and envy of his fellows.

"Question: Why does he crave admiration?

"Answer: Because, as a man, he is a social animal.

"Question: Why is Man a social animal?

"So go the questions and responses, expanding to infinity. Therefore—"

In a passion Hurtiancz leapt to his feet. Raising the brown glass pot above his head he dashed it to the floor. "Enough of this intolerable inanity! I propose that such loquacity passes beyond the scope of nuisance and over the verge of turpitude."

"It is a fine point," said Herark. "Ildefonse, what have you to say on this score?"

"I am more inclined to punish Hurtiancz for his crassness,"

said Ildefonse. "But now he simulates a swinish stupidity to escape my anger."

"Absolute falsity!" roared Hurtiancz. "I simulate nothing!"

Ildefonse shrugged. "For all his deficiencies as polemicist and magician, Hurtiancz at least is candid."

Hurtiancz controlled his fury. He said, "Who could defeat your volubility? As a magician however I outmatch your bumbling skills as Rhialto the Marvellous exceeds your rheumy decrepitude."

Ildefonse in his turn became angry. "A test!" He flung up his hand; the massive blocks scattered in all directions; they stood on a vacant floor in the full glare of sunlight. "What of that?"

"Trivial," said Hurtiancz. "Match this!" He held up his two hands; from each finger issued a jet of vivid smoke, in ten different colors.

"The petty prank of a charlatan," declared Ildefonse. "Now watch! I utter a word: 'Roof'!" The word leaving his lips hesitated in the air, in the form of symbol, then moved out in a wide circle, to impinge upon the roof of one of the strangely styled structures still extant. The symbol disappeared; the roof glowed a vivid orange and melted to spawn a thousand symbols like the word Ildefonse had sent forth. These darted high in the sky, stopped short, disappeared. From above, like a great clap of thunder, came Ildefonse's voice: "ROOF!"

"No great matter," stated Hurtiancz. "Now—"

"Hist!" said Mune the Mage. "Cease your drunken quarrel. Look yonder!"

From the structure whose roof Ildefonse had demolished came a man.

9

THE MAN stood in the doorway. He was impressively tall. A long white beard hung down his chest; white hair covered his ears; his eyes glittered black. He wore an elegant caftan, woven in patterns of dark red, brown, black and blue. Now he stepped forward, and it could be seen that he trailed a cloud of glowing objects. Gilgad, who had returned from the plaza, instantly set up a shout: "The IOUN stones!"

The man came forward. His face showed an expression of calm inquiry. Ildefonse muttered, "It is Morreion! Of this there can be no doubt. The stature, the stance—they are unmistakable!"

"It is Morreion," Rhialto agreed. "But why is he so calm, as if each week he received visitors who took off his roof, as if 'Nothing' loomed over someone else?"

"His perceptions may have become somewhat dulled," Herark suggested. "Notice: he evinces no signal of human recognition."

Morreion came slowly forward, the IOUN stones swirling in his wake. The magicians gathered before the marble steps of the palace. Vermoulian stepped forth and raised his hand. "Hail, Morreion! We have come to take you from this intolerable isolation!"

Morreion looked from one face to the other. He made a guttural sound, then a rasping croak, as if trying organs whose use he had long forgotten.

Ildefonse now presented himself. "Morreion, my comrade! It is I, Ildefonse; do you not remember the old days at Kammerbrand? Speak then!"

"I hear," croaked Morreion. "I speak; but I do not remember."

Vermoulian indicated the marble stairs. "Step aboard, if you will; we depart this bleak and dreary world at once."

44

Morreion made no move. He examined the palace with a frown of vexation. "You have placed your flying hut upon the area where I dry my skeins."

Ildefonse pointed off toward the black wall, which through the haze of the atmosphere showed only as a portentous shadow. " 'Nothing' looms close. It is about to impinge upon this world, whereupon you will be no more; in short, you will be dead."

"I am not clear as to your meaning," said Morreion. "If you will excuse me, I must be away and about my affairs."

"A quick question before you go," spoke Gilgad. "Where does one find IOUN stones?"

Morreion looked at him without comprehension. At last he gave his attention to the stones, which swirled with a swifter motion. In comparison, those of the archveult Xexamedes were listless and dull. These danced and curveted, and sparkled with different colors. Closest to Morreion's head moved the lavender and the pale green stones, as if they thought themselves the most loved and most privileged. Somewhat more wayward were the stones glowing pink and green together; then came stones of a proud pure pink; then the Royal carmine stones; then the red and blue; and finally, at the outer periphery, a number of stones glittering with intense blue lights.

As Morreion cogitated, the magicians noted a peculiar circumstance: certain of the innermost lavender stones lost their glow and became as dull as the stones of Xexamedes.

Morreion gave a slow thought nod. "Curious! So much which I seem to have forgotten. . . . I did not always live here," he said in a voice of surprise. "There was at one time another place. The memory is dim and remote."

Vermoulian said, "That place is Earth! It is where we will take you."

Morreion smilingly shook his head. "I am just about to start on an important journey."

"Is the trip absolutely necessary?" inquired Mune the Mage.

"Our time is limited, and even more to the point, we do not care to be engulfed in 'Nothing'."

"I must see to my cairns," said Morreion in a mild but definite manner.

For a moment there was silence. Then Ildefonse asked, "What is the purpose of these cairns?"

Morreion used the even voice of one speaking to a child. "They indicate the most expeditious route around my world. Without the cairns it is possible to go astray."

"But remember, there is no longer need for such landmarks," said Ao of the Opals. "You will be returning to Earth with us!"

Morreion could not restrain a small laugh at the obtuse persistence of his visitors. "Who would look after my properties? How would I fare if my cairns toppled, if my looms broke, if my kilns crumbled, if my other enterprises dissolved, and all for the lack of methodical care?"

Vermoulian said blandly, "At least come aboard the palace to share our evening banquet."

"It will be my pleasure," replied Morreion. He mounted the marble steps, to gaze with pleasure around the pavilion. "Charming. I must consider something of this nature as a forecourt for my new mansion."

"There will be insufficient time," Rhialto told him.

" 'Time'?" Morreion frowned as if the word were unfamiliar to him. Other of the lavender stones suddenly went pale. "Time indeed! But time is required to do a proper job! This gown for instance." He indicated his gorgeously patterned caftan. "The weaving required four years. Before that I gathered beast-fur for ten years; then for another two years I bleached and dyed and spun. My cairns were built a stone at a time, each time I wandered around the world. My wanderlust has waned somewhat, but I occasionally make the journey, to rebuild where necessary, and to note the changes of the landscape."

Rhialto pointed to the sun. "Do you recognize the nature of that object?"

46

Morreion frowned. "I call it 'the sun'—though why I have chosen this particular term escapes me."

"There are many such suns," said Rhialto. "Around one of them swings that ancient and remarkable world which gave you birth. Do you remember Earth?"

Morreion looked dubiously up into the sky. "I have seen none of these other suns you describe. At night my sky is quite dark; there is no other light the world over save the glow of my fires. It is a peaceful world indeed. . . . I seem to recall more eventful times." The last of the lavender stones and certain of the green stones lost their color. Morreion's eyes became momentarily intent. He went to inspect the tame water nymphs which sported in the central fountain. "And what might be these glossy little creatures? They are most appealing."

"They are quite fragile, and useful only as show," said Vermoulian. "Come, Morreion, my valet will help you prepare for the banquet."

"You are most gracious," said Morreion.

10

THE MAGICIANS awaited their guest in the grand salon. Each had his own opinion of the circumstances. Rhialto said, "Best that we raise the palace now and so be off and away. Morreion may be agitated for a period, but when all the facts are laid before him, he must surely see reason."

The cautious Perdustin demurred. "There is power in the man! At one time, his magic was a source of awe and wonder; what if in a fit of pique he wreaks a harm upon all of us?"

Gilgad endorsed Perdustin's view. "Everyone has noted Morreion's IOUN stones. Where did he acquire them? Can this world be the source?"

"Such a possibility should not automatically be dismissed," admitted Ildefonse. "Tomorrow, when the imminence of 'Nothing' is described, Morreion will surely depart without resentment."

So the matter rested. The magicians turned their discussion to other aspects of this dismal world.

Herark the Harbinger, who had skill as a cognizancer, attempted to divine the nature of the race which had left ruins across the planet, without notable success. "They have been gone too long; their influence has waned. I seem to discern creatures with thin white legs and large green eyes. . . . I hear a whisper of their music: a jingling, a tinkle, to a rather plaintive obligato of pipes. . . . I sense no magic. I doubt if they recognized the IOUN stones, if in fact such exist on this planet."

"Where else could they originate?" demanded Gilgad.

"The 'shining fields' are nowhere evident," remarked Haze of Wheary Water.

Morreion entered the hall. His appearance had undergone a dramatic change. The great white beard had been shaved away; his bush of hair had been cropped to a more modish style. In the place of his gorgeous caftan he wore a garment of ivory silk with a blue sash and a pair of scarlet slippers. Morreion now stood revealed as a tall spare man, attentive and alert. Glittering black eyes dominated his face, which was taut, harsh at chin and jaw, massive of forehead, disciplined in the even line of the mouth. The lethargy and boredom of so many aeons were nowhere evident; he moved with easy command, and behind him, darting and circling, swarmed the IOUN stones.

Morreion greeted the assembled magicians with an inclination of the head, and gave his attention to the appointments of the salon. "Magnificent and luxurious! But I will be forced to use quartz in the place of this splendid marble, and there is little silver to be found; the Sahars plundered all the surface ores. When I need metal I must tunnel deep underground."

"You have led a busy existence," declared Ildefonse. "And who were the Sahars?"

"The race whose ruins mar the landscape. A frivolous and irresponsible folk, though I admit that I find their poetic conundrums amusing."

"The Sahars still exist?"

"Indeed not! They became extinct long ages ago. But they left numerous records etched on bronze, which I have taken occasion to translate."

"A tedious job, surely!" exclaimed Zilifant. "How did you achieve so complicated a task?"

"By the process of elimination," Morreion explained. "I tested a succession of imaginary languages against the inscriptions, and in due course I found a correspondence. As you say, the task was time-consuming; still I have had much entertainment from the Sahar chronicles. I want to orchestrate their musical revelries; but this is a task for the future, perhaps after I complete the palace I now intend."

Ildefonse spoke in a grave voice, "Morreion, it becomes necessary to impress certain important matters upon you. You state that you have not studied the heavens?"

"Not extensively," admitted Morreion. "There is little to be seen save the sun, and under favorable conditions a great wall of impenetrable blackness."

"That wall of blackness," said Ildefonse, "is 'Nothing', toward which your world is inexorably drifting. Any further work here is futile."

Morreion's black eyes glittered with doubt and suspicion. "Can you prove this assertion?"

"Certainly. Indeed we came here from Earth to rescue you."

Morreion frowned. Certain of the green stones abruptly lost their color. "Why did you delay so long?"

Ao of the Opals gave a bray of nervous laughter, which he quickly stifled. Ildefonse turned him a furious glare.

"Only recently were we made aware of your plight," explained

49

Rhialto. "Upon that instant we prevailed upon Vermoulian to bring us hither in his peregrine palace."

Vermoulian's bland face creased in displeasure. "'Prevailed' is not correct!" he stated. "I was already on my way when the others insisted on coming along. And now, if you will excuse us for a few moments, Morreion and I have certain important matters to discuss."

"Not so fast," Gilgad cried out. "I am equally anxious to learn the source of the stones."

Ildefonse said, "I will put the question in the presence of us all. Morreion, where did you acquire your IOUN stones?"

Morreion looked around at the stones. "To be candid, the facts are somewhat vague. I seem to recall a vast shining surface. . . . But why do you ask? They have no great usefulness. So many ideas throng upon me. It seems that I had enemies at one time, and false friends, I must try to remember."

Ildefonse said, "At the moment you are among your faithful friends, the magicians of Earth. And if I am not mistaken, the noble Vermoulian is about to set before us the noblest repast in any of our memories!"

Morreion said with a sour smile, "You must think my life that of a savage. Not so! I have studied the Sahar cuisine and improved upon it! The lichen which covers the plain may be prepared in at least one hundred and seventy fashions. The turf beneath is the home of succulent helminths. For all its drab monotony, this world provides a bounty. If what you say is true, I shall be sorry indeed to leave."

"The facts cannot be ignored," said Ildefonse. "The IOUN stones, so I suppose, derive from the northern part of this world?"

"I believe not."

"The southern area, then?"

"I rarely visit this section; the lichen is thin; the helminths are all gristle."

A gong-stroke sounded; Vermoulian ushered the company into the dining-room, where the great table glittered with silver and crystal. The magicians seated themselves under the five chandeliers; in deference to his guest who had lived so long in solitude, Vermoulian refrained from calling forth the beautiful women of ancient eras.

Morreion ate with caution, tasting all set before him, comparing the dishes to the various guises of lichen upon which he usually subsisted. "I had almost forgotten the existence of such food," he said at last. "I am reminded, dimly, of other such feasts—so long ago, so long. . . . Where have the years gone? Which is the dream?" As he mused, some of the pink and green stones lost their color. Morreion sighed. "There is much to be learned, much to be remembered. Certain faces here arouse flickering recollections; have I known them before?"

"You will recall all in due course," said the diabolist Shrue. "And now, if we are certain that the IOUN stones are not to be found on this planet—"

"But we are not sure!" snapped Gilgad. "We must seek, we must search; no effort is too arduous!"

"The first to be found necessarily will go to satisfy my claims," declared Rhialto. "This must be a definite undertaking."

Gilgad thrust his vulpine face forward. "What nonsense is this? Your claims were satisfied by a choice from the effects of the archveult Xexamedes!"

Morreion jerked around. "The archveult Xexamedes! I know the name. . . . How? Where. . . . Long ago I knew an archveult Xexamedes; he was my foe, or so it seems. . . . Ah, the ideas which roil my mind!" The pink and green stones all had lost their color; Morreion groaned and put his hands to his head. "Before you came my life was placid; you have brought me doubt and wonder."

"Doubt and wonder are the lot of all men," said Ildefonse. "Magicians are not excluded. Are you ready to leave Sahar Planet?"

Morreion sat looking into a goblet of wine. "I must collect my books. They are all I wish to take away."

11

MORREION CONDUCTED the magicians about his premises. The structures which had seemed miraculous survivals had in fact been built by Morreion, after one or another mode of the Sahar architecture. He displayed his three looms: the first for fine weaves, linens and silks; the second where he contrived patterned cloths; the third where his heavy rugs were woven. The same structure housed vats, dyes, bleaches and mordants. Another building contained the glass cauldron, as well as the kilns where Morreion produced earthenware pots, plates, lamps and tiles. His forge in the same building showed little use. "The Sahars scoured the planet clean of ores. I mine only what I consider indispensable, which is not a great deal."

Morreion took the group to his library, in which were housed many Sahar originals as well as books Morreion had written and illuminated with his own hands: translations of the Sahar classics, an encyclopedia of natural history, ruminations and speculations, a descriptive geography of the planet, with appended maps. Vermoulian ordered his staff to transfer the articles to the palace.

Morreion turned a last look around the landscape he had known so long and had come to love; then without a word he went to the palace and climbed the marble steps. In a subdued mood the magicians followed. Vermoulian went at once to the control belvedere, where he performed rites of buoyancy; the palace floated up from the final planet.

Ildefonse gave an exclamation of shock. "'Nothing' is close at hand—more imminent than we had suspected!"

The black wall loomed startlingly near; the last star and its single world drifted at the very brink.

"The perspectives are by no means clear," said Ildefonse. "There is no sure way of judging but it seems that we left not an hour too soon."

"Let us wait and watch," suggested Herark. "Morreion can learn our good faith for himself."

So the palace hung in space, with the pallid light of the doomed sun playing upon the five crystal spires, projecting long shadows behind the magicians where they stood by the balustrade.

The Sahar world was first to encounter 'Nothing'. It grazed against the enigmatic non-substance, then, urged by a component of orbital motion, a quarter of the original sphere moved out clear and free: a mound-like object with a precisely flat base, where the hitherto secret strata, zones, folds, intrusions and core were displayed to sight. . . . The sun reached 'Nothing'; it touched, advanced, it became a half-orange on a black mirror, then sank away from reality. Darkness shrouded the palace.

In the belvedere Vermoulian indited symbols on the mandate wheel. He struck them off, then put double fire to the speed-incense. The palace glided away, back toward the star-clouds.

Morreion turned away from the balustrade and went into the great hall, where he sat deep in thought.

Gilgad presently approached him. "Perhaps you have recalled the source of the IOUN stones?"

Morreion rose to his feet. He turned his level black eyes upon Gilgad, who stepped back a pace. The pink and green stones had long become pallid, and many of the pink as well.

Morreion's face was stern and cold. "I recall much! There was a cabal of enemies who tricked me—but all is as dim as the film of stars which hangs across far space. In some fashion, the stones are part and parcel of the matter. Why do you evince so large an interest in stones? Were you one of my former enemies? Is this the case with all of you? If so beware! I am a mild man, until I encounter antagonism."

The diabolist Shrue spoke soothingly. "We are not your enemies! Had we not lifted you from Sahar Planet, you would now be with 'Nothing'. Is this not proof?"

Morreion gave a grim nod; but he no longer seemed the mild and affable man they had first encountered.

To restore the previous amiability, Vermoulian hastened to the room of faded mirrors where he maintained his vast collection of beautiful women, in the form of matrices. These could be activated into corporeality by a simple anti-negative incantation; and presently from the room, one after the other, stepped those delightful confections of the past which Vermoulian had seen fit to revivify. On each occasion they came forth fresh, without recollection of previous manifestations; each appearance was new, no matter how affairs had gone before.

Among those whom Vermoulian had called forth was the graceful Mersei. She stepped into the grand salon, blinking in the bewilderment common to those evoked from the past. She stopped short in amazement, then with quick steps ran forward. "Morreion! What do you do here? They told us you had gone against the archveults, that you had been killed! By the Sacred Ray, you are sound and whole!"

Morreion looked down at the young woman in perplexity. The pink and red stones wheeled around his head. "Somewhere I have seen you, somewhere I have known you."

"I am Mersei! Do you not remember? You brought me a red rose growing in a porcelain vase. Oh, what have I done with it? I always keep it near. . . . But where am I? Where is the rose? No matter. I am here and you are here."

Ildefonse muttered to Vermoulian, "An irresponsible act, in my judgment; why were you not more cautious?"

Vermoulian pursed his lips in vexation. "She stems from the waning of the Forty-third Aeon; but I had not anticipated anything like this!"

"I suggest that you call her back into your room of matrices and there reduce her. Morreion seems to be undergoing a period of

54

instability; he needs peace and quietude; best not to introduce stimulations so unpredictable."

Vermoulian strolled across the room. "Mersei, my dear; would you be good enough to step this way?"

Mersei cast him a dubious look, then beseeched Morreion: "Do you not know me? Something is very strange; I can understand nothing of this; it is like a dream. Morreion, am I dreaming?"

"Come, Mersei," said Vermoulian suavely. "I wish a word with you."

"Stop!" spoke Morreion. "Magician, stand back; this fragrant creature is something which once I loved, at a time far gone."

The girl cried in a poignant voice: "A time far gone. It was no more than yesterday! I tended the sweet red rose, I looked at the sky; they had sent you to Jangk, by the red star Kerkaju, the Eye of the Polar Ape. And now you are here, and I am here. . . . What does it mean?"

"Inadvisable, inadvisable," muttered Ildefonse. He called out, "Morreion, this way, if you will. I see a curious concatenation of galaxies; perhaps here is the new home of the Sahars."

Morreion put his hand to the girl's shoulder. He looked into her face. "The sweet red rose blooms, and forever. . . . We are among magicians and strange events occur." He glanced aside at Vermoulian, then back to Mersei. "At this moment, go with Vermoulian the Dream-walker, who will show you to your chamber."

"Yes, dear Morreion, but when will I see you again? You look so strange, so strained and old, and you speak so peculiarly. . . ."

"Go now, Mersei. I must confer with Ildefonse."

Vermoulian led Mersei back toward the room of matrices. At the door she hesitated and looked back over her shoulder, but Morreion had already turned away. She followed Vermoulian into the room of matrices. The door closed behind them.

Morreion walked out on the pavilion, past the dark lime trees with their silver fruit, and leaned upon the balustrade. The sky was still dark, although ahead and below a few vagrant galaxies could now be seen. Morreion put his hand to his head; the pink stones and certain of the red stones lost their color.

Morreion swung around toward Ildefonse and those other magicians who had silently come out on the pavilion. He stepped forward, the IOUN stones tumbling one after the other in their hurry to keep up. Some were yet red, some showed shifting glints of blue and red, some burnt a cold incandescent blue. All the others had become the color of pearl. One of these drifted in front of Morreion's eyes; he caught it, gave it a moment of frowning inspection, then tossed it into the air. Spinning and jerking, with color momentarily restored, it was quick to rejoin the others, like a child embarrassed.

"Memory comes and goes," mused Morreion. "I am unsettled, in mind and heart. Faces drift before my eyes; they fade once more; other events move into a region of clarity. The archveults, the IOUN stones—I know something of these, though much is dim and murky, so best that I hold my tongue—"

"By no means!" declared Ao of the Opals. "We are interested in your experiences."

"To be sure!" said Gilgad.

Morreion's mouth twisted in a smile that was both sardonic and harsh, and also somewhat melancholy. "Very well, I tell this story, then, as if I were telling a dream.

"It seems that I was sent to Jangk on a mission—perhaps to learn the provenance of the IOUN stones? Perhaps. I hear whispers which tell me so much; it well may be. . . . I arrived at Jangk; I recall the landscape well. I remember a remarkable castle hollowed from an enormous pink pearl. In this castle I confronted the archveults. They feared me and stood back, and when I stated my wishes there was no demur. They would indeed take me to gather stones and so we set out, flying through space in an equipage, whose nature I cannot recall. The archveults were silent and watched me from the side of their eyes; then they became affable and I wondered at their mirth. But I felt no fear. I knew all their magic; I carried counter-spells at my fingernails, and at need could

56

fling them off instantly. So we crossed space, with the archveults laughing and joking in what I considered an insane fashion. I ordered them to stop. They halted instantly and sat staring at me.

"We arrived at the edge of the universe, and came down upon a sad cinder of a world, a dreadful place. Here we waited, in a region of burnt-out star-hulks, some still hot, some cold, some cinders like the world on which we stood—perhaps it too was a dead star. Occasionally we saw the corpses of dwarf stars, glistening balls of stuff so heavy that a speck outweighs an Earthly mountain. I saw such objects no more than ten miles across, containing the matter of a sun like vast Kerkaju. Inside these dead stars, the archveults told me, were to be found the IOUN stones. And how were they to be won, I asked? Must we drive a tunnel into that gleaming surface? They gave mocking calls of laughter at my ignorance; I uttered a sharp reprimand; instantly they fell silent. The spokesman was Xexamedes. From him I learned that no power known to man or magician could mar stuff so dense! We must wait.

" 'Nothing' loomed across the distance. Often the derelict hulks swung close in their orbits. The archveults kept close watch; they pointed and calculated, they carped and fretted; at last one of the shining balls struck across 'Nothing', expunging half of itself. When it swung out and away the archveults took their equipage down to the flat surface. All now ventured forth, with most careful precaution; unprotected from gravity a man instantly becomes as no more than an outline upon the surface. With slide-boards immune to gravity we traversed the surface.

"What a wonderful sight! 'Nothing' had wrought a flawless polish; for fifteen miles this mirrored plain extended, marred only at the very center by a number of black pock-marks. Here the IOUN stones were to be found, in nests of black dust.

"To win the stones is no small task. The black dust, like the slide-boards, counters gravity. It is safe to step from the slide-boards to the dust, but a new precaution must be taken. While the dust negates the substance below, other celestial objects suck, so one must use an anchor to hold himself in place. The archveults drive small barbed hooks into the dust, and tie themselves down with a cord, and this I did as well. By means of a special tool the dust is probed: a tedious task! The dust is packed tightly! Nevertheless, with great energy I set to work and in due course won my first IOUN stone. I held it high in exultation, but where were the archveults? They had circled around me; they had returned to the equipage! I sought my slide-boards—in vain! By stealth they had been purloined!

"I staggered, I sagged; I raved a spell at the traitors. They held forward their newly won IOUN stones; the magic was absorbed, as water entering a sponge.

"With no further words, no even signals of triumph—for this is how lightly they regarded me—they entered their equipage and were gone. In this region contiguous with 'Nothing', my doom was certain: so they were assured."

As Morreion spoke the red stones went pale; his voice quavered with a passion he had not hitherto displayed.

"I stood alone," said Morreion hoarsely. "I could not die, with the Spell of Untiring Nourishment upon me, but I could not move a step, not an inch from the cavity of black dust, or I would instantly have been no more than a print upon the surface of the shining field.

"I stood rigid—how long I cannot say. Years? Decades? I cannot remember. This period seems a time of dull daze. I searched my mind for resources, and I grew bold with despair. I probed for IOUN stones, and I won those which now attend me. They became my friends and gave me solace.

"I embarked then upon a new task, which, had I not been mad with despair, I would never have attempted. I brought up particles of black dust, I wet them with blood to make a paste; this paste I molded into a circular plate four feet in diameter.

"It was finished. I stepped aboard; I anchored myself with the barbed pins, and I floated up and away from the half-star.

"I had won free! I stood on my disk in the void! I was free, but I was alone. You cannot know what I felt until you too have stood in space, without knowledge of where to go. Far away I saw a single star, a rogue, a wanderer; toward this star I fared.

"How long the voyage required, again I cannot say. When I judged that I had traveled half-way, I turned the disk about and slowed my motion.

"Of this voyage I remember little. I spoke to my stones, I gave them my thoughts. I seemed to become calm from talking, for during the first hundred years of this voyage I felt a prodigious fury that seemed to overwhelm all rational thought; to inflict but a pin prick upon a single one of my adversaries I would have died by torture a hundred times! I plotted delicious vengeances, I became yeasty and exuberant upon the imagined pain I would inflict. Then at times I suffered unutterable melancholy—while others enjoyed the good things of life, the feasts, the comradeship, the caresses of their loved ones—here stood I, alone in the dark. The balance would be restored, I assured myself. My enemies would suffer as I had suffered, and more! . . . But the passion waned, and as my stones grew to know me they assumed their beautiful colors. Each has his name; each is individual; I know each stone by its motion. The archveults consider them the brain-eggs of fire-folk who live within these stars; as to this I cannot say.

"At last I came down upon my world. I had burned away my rage; I was calm and placid, as now you know me. My old lust for revenge I saw to be futility. I turned my mind to a new existence, and over the aeons I built my buildings and my cairns; I lived my new life.

"The Sahars excited my interest. I read their books, I learned their lore. . . . Perhaps I began to live a dream. My old life was far away: a discordant trifle to which I gave ever less importance. I am amazed that the language of Earth returned to me as readily as it has. Perhaps the stones held my knowledge in trust, and extended it as the need came. Ah, my wonderful stones, what would I be without them?

"Now I am back among men. I know how my life has gone. There are still confused areas; in due course I will remember all."

Morreion paused to consider; several of the blue and scarlet stones went quickly dim. Morreion quivered, as if touched by galvanic essence; his cropped white hair seemed to bristle. He took a slow step forward; certain of the magicians made uneasy movements.

Morreion spoke in a new voice, one less reflective and reminiscent, with a harsh grating sound somewhere at its basis. "Now I will confide in you." He turned the glitter of his black eyes upon each face in turn. "I intimated that my rage had waned with the aeons; this is true. The sobs which lacerated my throat, the gnashing which broke my teeth, the fury which caused my brain to shudder and ache: all dwindled; for I had nothing with which to feed my emotions. After bitter reflection came tragic melancholy, then at last peace, which your coming disturbed.

"A new mood has now come upon me! As the past becomes real, so I have returned along the way of the past. There is a difference. I am now a cold cautious man; perhaps I can never experience the extremes of passion which once consumed me. On the other hand, certain periods of my life are still dim." Another of the red and scarlet stones lost its vivid glow; Morreion stiffened, his voice took on a new edge. "The crimes upon my person call out for rebuttal! The archveults of Jangk must pay in the fullest and most onerous measure! Vermoulian the Dream-walker, expunge the present symbols from your mandate wheel! Our destination now becomes the planet Jangk!"

Vermoulian looked to his colleagues to learn their opinion.

Ildefonse cleared his throat. "I suggest that our host Vermoulian first pause at Earth, to discharge those of us with urgent business. Those others will continue with Vermoulian and Morreion to Jangk; in this way the convenience of all may be served."

Morreion said in a voice ominously quiet: "No business is as urgent as mine, which already has been delayed too long." He spoke to Vermoulian: "Apply more fire to the speed-incense! Proceed directly to Jangk."

Haze of Wheary Water said diffidently, "I would be remiss if I failed to remind you that the archveults are powerful magicians; like yourself they wield IOUN stones."

Morreion made a furious motion; as his hand swept the air, it left a trail of sparks. "Magic derives from personal force! My passion alone will defeat the archveults! I glory in the forthcoming confrontation. Ah, but they will regret their deeds!"

"Forbearance has been termed the noblest of virtues," Ildefonse suggested. "The archveults have long forgotten your very existence; your vengeance will seem an unjust and unnecessary tribulation."

Morreion swung around his glittering black gaze. "I reject the concept. Vermoulian, obey!"

"We fare toward Jangk," said Vermoulian.

12

ON A MARBLE BENCH between a pair of silver-fruited lime trees sat Ildefonse. Rhialto stood beside him, one elegant leg raised to the bench: a posture which displayed his rose satin cape with the white lining to dramatic advantage. They drifted through a cluster of a thousand stars; great lights passed above, below, to each side; the crystal spires of the palace gave back millions of scintillations.

Rhialto had already expressed his concern at the direction of events. Now he spoke again, more emphatically. "It is all very well to point out that the man lacks facility; as he asserts, sheer force can overpower sophistication."

Ildefonse said bluffly, "Morreion's force is that of hysteria, diffuse and undirected."

"Therein lies the danger! What if by some freak his wrath focuses upon us?"

"Bah, what then?" demanded Ildefonse. "Do you doubt my ability, or your own?"

"The prudent man anticipates contingencies," said Rhialto with dignity. "Remember, a certain area of Morreion's life remains clouded."

Ildefonse tugged thoughtfully at his white beard. "The aeons have altered all of us; Morreion not the least of any."

"This is the core of my meaning," said Rhialto. "I might mention that not an hour since I essayed a small experiment. Morreion walked the third balcony, watching the stars pass by. His attention being diverted, I took occasion to project a minor spell of annoyance toward him: Houlart's Visceral Pang—but with no perceptible effect. Next I attempted the diminutive version of Lugwiler's Dismal Itch, again without success. I noted, however, his IOUN stones pulsed bright as they absorbed the magic. I tried my own Green Turmoil; the stones glowed bright, and this time Morreion became aware of the attention. By happy chance Byzant the Necrope passed by. Morreion put an accusation upon him, which Byzant denied. I left them engaged in contention. The instruction is this: first, Morreion's stones guard him from hostile magic; second, he is vigilant and suspicious; third, he is not one to shrug aside an offense."

Ildefonse nodded gravely. "We must certainly take these matters into consideration. I now appreciate the scope of Xexamedes' plan; he intended harm to all. . . . But behold in the sky yonder! Is that not the constellation Elektha, seen from obverse? We are in familiar precincts once more. Kerkaju must lie close ahead, and with it that extraordinary planet Jangk."

The two strolled to the forward part of the pavilion. "You are right!" exclaimed Rhialto. He pointed. "There is Kerkaju; I recognize its scarlet empharism!"

The planet Jangk appeared: a world with a curious dull sheen.

At Morreion's direction, Vermoulian directed the palace down to Smokedancers Bluff, at the southern shore of the Quicksilver Ocean. Guarding themselves against the poisonous air, the magicians descended the marble steps and walked out on the bluff, where an inspiring vista spread before them. Monstrous Kerkaju bulged across the green sky, every pore and flocculation distinct, with its simulacrum mirrored in the Quicksilver Ocean. Directly below, at the base of the bluff, quicksilver puddled and trickled across flats of black hornblende; here the Jangk "dragoons"—purple pansy-shaped creatures six feet in diameter—grazed on tufts of crystalline moss. Somewhat to the east the town Kaleshe descended in terraces to the shore.

Morreion, standing at the edge of the bluff, inhaled the noxious vapors which blew in from the ocean, as if they were a tonic. "My memory quickens," he called out. "I remember this scene as if it were yesterday. There have been changes, true. Yonder far peak has eroded to half its height; the bluffs on which we stand have been thrust upwards at least a hundred feet. Has it been so long? While I built my cairns and pored over my books the aeons flitted past. Not to mention the unknown period I rode through space on a disk of blood and star-stuff. . . . Let us proceed to Kaleshe; it was formerly the haunt of the archveult Persain."

"When you encounter your enemies, what then?" asked Rhialto. "Are your spells prepared and ready?"

"What need I for spells?" grated Morreion. "Behold!" He pointed his finger; a flicker of emotion spurted forth to shatter a boulder. He clenched his fists, the constricted passion crackled as if he had crumpled stiff parchment. He strode off toward Kaleshe, the magicians trooping behind.

The Kalsh had seen the palace descend; a number had gathered at the top of the bluff. Like the archveults they were sheathed in pale blue scales. Osmium cords constricted the black plumes of the men; the feathery green plumes of the women however waved and swayed as they walked. All stood seven feet tall, and were slim as lizards.

Morreion halted. "Persain, stand forth!" he called.

One of the men spoke: "There is no Persain at Kaleshe."

"What? No archveult Persain?"

"None of this name. The local archveult is a certain Evorix, who departed in haste at the sight of your peregrine palace."

"Who keeps the town records?"

Another Kalsh stepped forth. "I am that functionary."

"Are you acquainted with Persain the archveult?"

"I know by repute a Persain who was swallowed by a dragoon toward the end of the 47th Aeon."

Morreion uttered a groan. "Has he evaded me? What of Xexamedes?"

"He is gone from Jangk; no one knows where."

"Djorin?"

"He lives, but keeps to a pink pearl castle across the ocean."

"Aha! What of Ospro?"

"Dead."

Morreion gave another abysmal groan. "Vexel?"

"Dead."

Morreion groaned once more. Name by name he ran down the roster of his enemies. Four only survived.

When Morreion turned about his face had become haunted and haggard; he seemed not to see the magicians of Earth. All of his scarlet and blue stones had given up their color. "Four only," he muttered. "Four only to receive the charge of all my force. . . . Not enough, not enough! So many have won free! Not enough, not enough! The balance must adjust!" He made a brusque gesture. "Come! To the castle of Djorin."

In the palace they drifted across the ocean while the great red globe of Kerkaju kept pace above and below. Cliffs of mottled quartz and cinnabar rose ahead; on a crag jutting over the ocean stood a castle in the shape of a great pink pearl.

The peregrine palace settled upon a level area; Morreion leapt down the steps and advanced toward the castle. A circular door of solid osmium rolled back; an archveult nine feet tall, with black plumes waving three feet over his head, came forth.

Morreion called, "Send forth Djorin; I have dealings with him."

"Djorin is within! We have had a presentiment! You are the land-ape Morreion, from the far past. Be warned; we are prepared for you."

64

"Djorin!" called Morreion. "Come forth!"

"Djorin will not come forth," stated the archveult, "nor will Arvianid, Ishix or Herclamon, or the other archveults of Jangk who have come to combine their power against yours. If you seek vengeance, turn upon the real culprits; do not annoy us with your peevish complaints." The archveult returned within and the osmium door rolled shut.

Morreion stood stock-still. Mune the Mage came forward, and stated: "I will winkle them out, with Houlart's Blue Extractive." He hurled the spell toward the castle, to no effect. Rhialto attempted a spell of brain pullulations, but the magic was absorbed; Gilgad next brought down his Instantaneous Galvanic Thrust, which spattered harmlessly off the glossy pink surface.

"Useless," said Ildefonse. "Their IOUN stones absorb the magic."

The archveults in their turn became active. Three ports opened; three spells simultaneously issued forth, to be intercepted by Morreion's IOUN stones, which momentarily pulsed the brighter.

Morreion stepped three paces forward. He pointed his finger; force struck at the osmium door. It creaked and rattled, but held firm.

Morreion pointed his finger at the fragile pink nacre; the force slid away and was wasted.

Morreion pointed at the stone posts which supported the castle. They burst apart. The castle lurched, rolled over, and down the crags. It bounced from jut to jut, smashing and shattering, and splashed into the Quicksilver Ocean, where a current caught it and carried it out to sea. Through rents in the nacre the archveults crawled forth, to clamber to the top. More followed, until their accumulated weight rolled the pearl over, throwing all on top into the quicksilver sea, where they sank as deep as their thighs. Some tried to walk and leap to the shore, others lay flat on their backs and sculled with their hands. A gust of wind caught the pink bubble and sent it rolling across the sea, tossing off archveults as a turning wheel flings away drops of water. A band of Jangk "dragoons" put out from the shore, to envelop and devour the archveults closest at hand; the others allowed themselves to drift on the current and out to sea, where they were lost to view.

Morreion turned slowly toward the magicians of Earth. His face was gray. "A fiasco," he muttered. "It is nothing."

Slowly he walked toward the palace. At the steps he stopped short. "What did they mean: 'the real culprits'?"

"A figure of speech," replied Ildefonse. "Come up on the pavilion; we will refresh ourselves with wine. At last your vengeance is complete. And now. . . ." His voice died as Morreion climbed the steps. One of the bright blue stones lost its color. Morreion stiffened as if at a twinge of pain. He swung around, to look from magician to magician. "I remember a certain face: a man with a bald head; black beardlets hung from each of his cheeks. He was a burly man. . . . What was his name?"

"These events are far in the past," said the diabolist Shrue. "Best to put them out of mind."

Other blue stones became dull; Morreion's eyes seemed to assume the light they had lost.

"The archveults came to Earth; we conquered them; they begged for their lives. So much I recall. . . . The chief magician demanded the secret of the IOUN stones. Ah! What was his name? He had a habit of pulling on his black beardlets. . . . A handsome man, a great popinjay—I almost see his face—he made a proposal to the chief magician. Ah! Now it begins to come clear!" The blue stones faded one by one. Morreion's face shone with a white fire. The last of the blue stones went pallid.

Morreion spoke in a soft voice, a delicate voice, as if he savored each word. "The chief magician's name was Ildefonse. The popinjay was Rhialto. I remember each detail. Rhialto proposed that I go to learn the secret; Ildefonse vowed to protect me, as if I were his own life. I trusted them; I trusted all the magicians in the chamber: Gilgad was there, and Hurtiancz and Mune the Mage and Perdustin. All my dear friends, who joined in a solemn vow to make the archveults hostage for my safety. Now I know the culprits. The archveults dealt with me as an enemy. My friends sent me forth and never thought of me again. Ildefonse—what have you to say, before you go to wait out twenty aeons in a certain place of which I know?"

Ildefonse said bluffly, "Come, now, you must not take matters so seriously. All's well that ends well; we are now happily reunited and the secret of the IOUN stones is ours!"

"For each pang I suffered, you shall suffer twenty," said Morreion. "Rhialto as well, and Gilgad, and Mune, and Herark and all the rest. Vermoulian, lift the palace. Return us the way we have come. Put double fire to the incense."

Rhialto looked at Ildefonse who shrugged.

"Unavoidable," said Rhialto. He evoked the Spell of Temporal Stasis. Silence fell upon the scene. Each person stood like a monument.

Rhialto bound Morreion's arms to his side with swaths of tape. He strapped Morreion's ankles together, and wrapped bandages into Morreion's mouth, to prevent him uttering a sound. He found a net and capturing the IOUN stones drew them down about Morreion's head, in close contact with his scalp. As an afterthought he taped a blindfold over Morreion's eyes.

He could do no more. He dissolved the spell. Ildefonse was already walking across the pavilion. Morreion jerked and thrashed in disbelief. Ildefonse and Rhialto lowered him to the marble floor.

"Vermoulian," said Ildefonse, "be so good as to call forth your staff. Have them bring a trundle and convey Morreion to a dark room. He must rest for a spell."

13

RHIALTO FOUND his manse as he had left it, with the exception of the way-post, which was complete. Well satisfied, Rhialto went into one of his back rooms. Here he broke open a hole into subspace and placed therein the netful of IOUN stones which he carried. Some gleamed incandescent blue; others were mingled scarlet and blue; the rest shone deep red, pink, pink and green, pale green and pale lavender.

Rhialto shook his head ruefully and closed the dimension down upon the stones. Returning to his work-room he located Puiras among the Minuscules and restored him to size.

"Once and for all, Puiras, I find that I no longer need your services. You may join the Minuscules, or you may take your pay and go."

Puiras gave forth a roar of protest, "I worked my fingers to the bone; is this all the thanks I get?"

"I do not care to argue with you; in fact, I have already engaged your replacement."

Puiras eyed the tall vague-eyed man who had wandered into the work-room. "Is this the fellow? I wish him luck. Give me my money; and none of your magic gold, which goes to sand!"

Puiras took his money and went his way. Rhialto spoke to the new servitor. "For your first task, you may clear up the wreckage of the aviary. If you find corpses, drag them to the side; I will presently dispose of them. Next, the tile of the great hall. . . ."

OUR NEXT STORY is the work of Poul Anderson. Born in Bristol, Pennsylvania, in 1926, Poul graduated as a physics major from the University of Minnesota. He obviously intended to become a physicist, but Fate intervened: even while at college, he had sold his first few stories (to John Campbell), and upon graduating found himself already launched on the precarious but pleasurable career of a free-lance writer, which he has been ever since.

That shrewd critic, Damon Knight, once observed: "As a thinker, Anderson belongs to the rationalists; as a writer, to the romantics. The paradoxical combination is a powerful one." Very true—as the story that follows will bear out.

POUL is very popular and very prolific in science fiction, and you may know him through such good books as *The High Crusade* (1960) or *Brain Wave* (1954). He has probably written more science fiction than any other writer alive—Damon also observed that the Andersoniana published between 1950 and 1966 filled three solid pages of the M. I. T. Index. According to my own count (and I may well have missed a title or two), he has published at least forty-two books. Not at all a sparse record, for a writer only 44! Along the way Poul has garnered a few Hugo Awards, too.

Not all of those forty-two books are science fiction, of course. There are a couple of mysteries, an historical novel or two, a non-fiction volume on extraterrestrial life, a children's book—and two thoroughly entertaining novels of heroic fantasy, which we of S.A.G.A. count as his swordly and sorcerous credentials.

The earliest of these, *The Broken Sword* (1954), was a fantasy of the Viking age, and was also, I believe, Poul's very first book, hence, very likely, a labor of love. It has since been revised and republished in the Ballantine Adult Fantasy Series which I edit.

The second of his two major fantasies, *Three Hearts and Three Lions,* is laid in the imaginary world of Charlemagne's empire—the world invented by the authors of the Carolingian epics, that is, not the historical age of the actual Frankish emperor—and it is concerned with the adventures of a hero who turns out to be a modern reincarnation of Ogier the Dane. It is simply a splendid book. And it also has recently been reissued.

Anderson comes by his interest in the Vikings and their saga-literature and heroic mythology legitimately, as he is of Danish ancestry and can read Old Norse. (I know he can, because for years now the Sword & Sorcery fanzine, *Amra,* has been publishing his occasional verse translations from that obscure language.)

Two fantasies out of a total of forty-two books does not exactly suggest that Poul is a dyed-in-the-wool Sword & Sorcery buff, I admit. But such is, in fact, the truth; I believe the numerical discrepancy arose from the fact that Poul has long since been typed by editors and publishers as a reliable author of science fiction *per se,* and thus it is only his science fiction they want to see. Thus he must concentrate on sf, to the neglect of S&S, which he would probably prefer writing.

As proof of this, let me quote from a postcard I received from Poul in reply to my request for a tale for this S.A.G.A. anthology. Poul wrote:

> "Dear Lin: With all else I have to get done before
> summer, it would be utter madness for me to agree
> to write 15,000 words of S&S. Therefore—
> YES! I'D BE *DELIGHTED!*"

To his tale, Poul adds this note: "Those who know the medieval ballad of Agnete and her lover will see that this story makes a

70

couple of changes. She is here supposed to have borne him daughters as well as sons; and the setting has been moved from England to Denmark. This was done not only for the sake of narrative, but for plausibility. Seven boys in a row is unlikely if not impossible; and the poem is purely Danish. Over the centuries the legend must have assumed what form looked most glamorous to the people. I hope my own use has kept the spirit of it."

The Merman's Children

by POUL ANDERSON

1

THE bishop of Viborg got Magnus Gregersen for his new archdeacon. This man was more learned than most, having studied in Paris, and he was upright and pious; but folk called him too strict, and said they liked no better to see him coming, with his long lean frame and his long sour face, than they liked to see any other black crow in their fields. The bishop felt one like that was needed, for laxity had set in during the years of strife that harried Denmark after King Erik Plowpenny died.

Riding along the eastern Jutish coast as episcopal provost, Magnus came to Als, not the island but a hamlet of the same name. It was poor and lonely, cut off to south and west by deep woods through which ran but a pair of roads, to north by Kongerslev Marsh, and to east by the Kattegat. Each September and October its fishermen would join the thousands that made catches in the Sound during the great herring run; otherwise their kind saw little of the outside world. They dragged their nets along the coast and farmed their thin-soiled acres until time and toil broke them and they laid their bones to rest behind the small wooden church. Many old ways were still followed in steads like this. Magnus thought such doings heathenish and bewailed to himself that there was no ready way to stop them.

Thus a baffled zeal grew doubly strong in him when he heard certain rumors about Als. None there would own to knowledge of what might have been happening since that day fourteen years ago when Agnete came back out of the sea. Magnus got the priest alone and sternly demanded the truth. Father Knud was a gentle man, born in one of these tiny houses, who had long turned a blind eye on what he thought were minor sins that gave his flock some cheer in their bleak lives. But he was old now, and feeble, and Magnus soon wrung from him the full tale.

The provost returned to Viborg with a holy flame in his eyes. He went to the bishop and said: "My lord, in making my round through your diocese I found woefully many signs of the devil's work. But I had not looked to come upon himself—no, say rather a whole nest of his foulest, most dangerous fiends. Yet this I did in the strand-hamlet Als."

"What mean you?" asked the bishop sharply; for he also dreaded a return of the old witchy gods.

"I mean that offshore is a town of merfolk!"

The bishop eased. "How interesting," he said. "I knew not that any were left in Danish waters. They are not devils, my good Magnus. They lack souls, yes, like other beasts. But they do not imperil salvation as might the dwellers in an elfhill. Indeed, they seldom have aught to do with the tribe of Adam."

"These are otherwise, my lord," answered the archdeacon. "Listen to what I have learned. Two and twenty years ago lived near Als a maiden hight Agnete Einarsdatter. Her father was a yeoman, well-to-do by his neighbors' reckoning, and she was very fair, so she ought to have made a good marriage. But one eventide when she walked alone on the strand, a merman trod forth and wooed her. He lured her away with him, and she passed eight years in sin and godlessness beneath the sea.

"At last she happened to bring her newest babe up onto a skerry that it might drink sunlight. This was in earshot of the church bells, and while she sat rocking the cradle, they began to chime. Home-sickness, if not repentance, awoke in her. She went to the merman and begged leave to go hear again the word of God. He gave unwilling consent and took her ashore. Beforehand he made her vow not to do three things—let down her long hair, as if she were unwedded; seek out her mother in the family pew; and bow down when the priest named the All Highest. But each of these she did: the first for pride, the second for love, the third for awe. Then divine grace drew the scales from her eyes and she stayed on land.

"Afterward the merman came in search of her. It was another holy day and he found her at mass. When he walked into the church, the pictures and images turned their faces to the wall. None of the congregation dared lift hand against him, for he was huge and strong and so heavy that he had left a track behind him even though it was summer and the street dry. He pleaded with her to come, he spoke of their children that wept for her, and well might he have prevailed as aforetime. For this is not a hideous race with fish tails, my lord. Save that they have broad, webbed feet and big, slanting eyes, and the men among them are beardless, and some have green or blue hair—on the whole, they look like beautiful humans. His own locks were golden as hers. And he did not threaten, he spoke in tones of love and sorrow.

"Yet God strengthened Agnete. She refused him and he went back beneath the waters.

"Her father had the prudence, and the dowry, to get her wed inland. They say she was never cheerful, and before long she died."

"If it was a Christian death," the bishop said, "I cannot see that lasting harm was done."

"But the merfolk are still there, my lord!" cried the provost. "Fishermen see them often, romping and laughing in the waves. Does that not make a poor toiler, who dwells in a wretched hut with an ugly wife, ill content, yes, even questioning of God's justice? And when will another merman seduce another maiden, this time forever? That is the more likely now when those children of Agnete and her lover are grown. They come ashore almost as a habit, and are striking up friendships with some of the boys and young men—worse, with some of the girls.

"My lord, this is Satan's work! If we let souls be lost that were in our charge, how shall we answer on the Last Day?"

The bishop scowled and rubbed his chin. "You have right. What shall we try, though? If the Alsmen already do what is forbidden, a further ban will hardly check them; I know those stiff-necked fisher folk. And if we send to the king for knights and soldiers, how shall they go beneath the sea?"

Magnus raised a finger. It blazed from him: "My lord, I have studied matters of this kind and know the cure. Those merfolk may not be demons, but the soulless must ever flee when God's word is properly laid on them. Have I your leave to conduct an exorcism?"

"You do," said the bishop shakenly, "and with it my blessing."

So it came about that Magnus returned to Als. More men-at-arms than usual clattered behind him, lest the villagers make trouble. They watched, some eager for any newness, some surly, a few weeping, as the archdeacon had himself rowed out to a spot above the underwater town. And there, with bell, book, and candle, he solemnly cursed the sea people and bade them in God's name forever be gone.

2

TAUNO, oldest child of fair Agnete and the Liri king, had counted his twenty-first winter. There was great merrymaking in his honor, feast, song, dances that wove their flitting patterns north, east, west, south, up, down, and around, between the shells and mirrors and golden plates which flung back the seafire lighting the royal hall; there were gifts, cunningly wrought, not alone of gold and amber and narwhal ivory, but also of pearl and lacy rosy coral, brought from afar by dolphin caravans; there were contests in swimming, wrestling, harpooning, music, and runecraft; there was lovemaking in dim rooms which had no roof because none was needed, and in the rippling gardens of green and brown weed where tame fish darted like meteors.

Afterward Tauno went on a long hunt. Though the merfolk lived off the sea, he fared this time in sport, and indeed mostly to visit anew the grandeur of the Norway fjords. With him came the girls Rinna and Raxi, for his pleasure and their own. They had a joyful trip, which meant much to Tauno; he was often a sober one among the lighthearted merfolk, and sometimes fell into dark broodings.

They were homebound, Liri was in sight, when the wrath struck them.

"Yonder it is!" Rinna called eagerly. She darted ahead. The green tresses streamed down her slim white back. Raxi stayed near Tauno. She swam laughing around and around him; as she passed below, she would stroke fingers over his face or loins. He grabbed for her with the same playfulness, but always she was out of reach. "Niaah!" she taunted while blowing him kisses. He grinned and swam steadily on. Having inherited their mother's shape of foot, the halfling children were less swift and deft in the water than their father's race. Nevertheless, a landman would have gasped at their movement. And they got about more readily on shore than their cousins; and they had been born able to live undersea, without need for the spells that had kept their mother from death by drawning, salt, or chill; and the cool-fleshed merfolk liked to embrace their warmer bodies.

Above Tauno sun smote waves, making a roof of bright ripples that traced itself across the white sand beneath him. Around, the water reached in hues of emerald and amethyst until distance brought dusk. He felt it slide by, answering the play of his muscles with caresses like a lover's. Kelp streamed upward from barnacled rocks, golden-brown, swaying to every current. A crab clanked over the seabed; a tunny glided further off, blue and white and splendid. The water was never the same: here cold, there mild, here roiled, there calm, and a thousand different tastes and odors

76

beyond the tang men smell on a strand; and it was full of sounds for those who could hear, cluckings, chucklings, croakings, chitterings, splashings, the hush-hush-hush where it lapped against land; and beneath each swirl and gurgle Tauno felt the huge slow striding of the tides.

Now Liri rose clear in his sight: houses that were hardly more than arbors of seaplants on frames of ivory and whale ribs, delicate and fantastically scrimshawed in this world of low weight, wide-spaced among gardens of weed and anemone; in the middle, the hall of his father the king, big, ancient, stone and coral in subtle hues, bedight with carven figures of fish and those beasts and fowl which belong to the sea. The posts of the main door were in the shapes of Lord Ægir and Lady Ran, the lintel was an albatross with wings spread for soaring. Above walls lifted a dome of crystal, vented to the surface, the king had let build for Agnete, so that when she wished she might be dry, breathe air, sit by a fire among roses and what else his love could fetch her from the land.

The merfolk flitted about—gardeners, craftsmen, a hunter training a brace of young seals, a whale herder buying a trident at a booth, a boy leading a girl by the hand toward some softly lighted cavern. Bronze bells, taken long ago from a wrecked ship, were being chimed; they pealed more clearly through water than ever through the air.

"Harroo!" Tauno shouted. He plunged forward in a burst of speed. Rinna and Raxi fell in alongside him. The three broke into the Song of Returnings he had made for them:

"Here may I hail you, my homeland, my heartstrand.
Well for the wanderer's weal is the way's end.
Call up the clamor on conchs and on kettles!
Stories I'll strew from the silver-paved swanroad.
Gold the dawn glittered and gay wheeled the gulls when—"

Suddenly the two girls screamed. They clapped hands to ears, their eyes were shut, they milled about blindly and wildly kicking till the water seethed.

Tauno watched that same craziness grab all of Liri. "What is this?" he cried in horror. "What's wrong?"

Rinna wailed her anguish. She could not see nor hear him. He caught her. She fought to break loose. His strength gripped her from behind with legs and one hand. His other hand closed in the long silken hair to hold tight her jerking head. He laid mouth to an ear and stammered, "Rinna, Rinna, it is me, Tauno. I am your friend. I want to help you."

"Then let me go!" Her shriek was ragged with pain and fright. "The ringing fills the sea, it shakes me like a shark, my bones are coming apart—the light, the cruel blaze, blinding, burning, burning —the words—Let me go or I die!"

Tauno did, altogether bewildered. Rising several yards, he made out the shivering shadow of a fisher boat, and heard a bell . . . was a fire aboard too, and was a voice chanting in some tongue he knew not? No more than that. . . .

The houses of Liri rocked as in a quake. The crystal dome on the hall shattered and rained down in a thousand bright shards. The stones trembled and began to slide from each other. That crumbling, of what had stood here since the Great Ice melted, sent its shuddering through Tauno's flesh.

Dimly he saw his father come forth, astride the orca which had its own airspace in the hall and which no one else dared mount. Otherwise the king had naught but a trident; and he was clad in naught but his own majesty. Yet somehow his call was heard: "To me, my people, to me! Quickly, before we die! Seek not to save any treasure beyond your children—come, come, come if you would live!"

Tauno shook Rinna and Raxi back to a measure of sense, and led them to join the throng. His father, riding about rallying the terrified merfolk, had time to say to him grimly: "You, half mortal, feel it no more than does this steed of mine. But to us, these waters are now banned. For us, the light will blaze and the bell will toll and the words will curse until the Weird of the World. We must flee while we still have strength, to seek a home far and far away."

"Where are my siblings?" Tauno asked.

"They were on an outing," said the king. The tone that had trumpeted went flat and dead. "We cannot wait for them."

"*I* can!"

The king gripped his son by both shoulders. "That gladdens me. Eyjan and Yria need more than young Kennin to ward them. I know not where we are going—maybe you can find us later, maybe—" He shook his sun-bright mane. His face drew into a mask of torture. "Away!" he screamed.

Stunned, beaten, naked, with hardly a tool or weapon among them, the merfolk followed their lord. Tauno hung, fists clenched on harpoon, until they were out of sight. The last stones of the royal hall toppled, and Liri was a ruin.

3

IN the eight years that she dwelt beneath the sea, fair Agnete bore seven children. This was less than a mermaid would have done, and maybe the unspoken scorn of those women helped drive her back to land, even as the bells of the little church and the sight of little thatch-roofed timber houses had drawn her.

For though the merfolk, like others of Faerie, knew no aging (as if He Whose name they did not speak thus repaid them for lack of immortal souls) their life had its harsh side. Shark, orca, sperm whale, ray, sea serpent, a dozen kinds of killer fish hunted them; the creatures that they in turn hunted were often dangerous; tricks of wind and wave could be deadly; poison fangs and spines, cold, sickness, hunger carried many off. This was most true of their young; they must reckon with losing all but a few. The king had been lucky. Behind his home were only three graves whereon the sea anemones had never been let die.

The four of his children who remained met in the wreckage of Liri. Round about were the heaped chaos of the hall, the further-off bits and pieces of lesser houses, gardens already withering, fishflocks already scattered, broken scrimshaw, crabs and lobsters swarming through foodstocks like ravens over a corpse on shore. The meeting spot was where the main door had been. The albatross lay wing-broken; kindly Lord Ægir had fallen on his face; Lady Ran who takes men in her nets stood above, grinning. The water was chill and waves raised by a storm overhead could be heard mourning for Liri.

The merman's children were unclad, as was the custom undersea save at festival times. However, they had gotten knives, harpoons, tridents, and axes of stone and bone, to ward off those menaces which circled closer and closer beyond the rim of their sight. None of them looked wholly like merfolk. But the elder three shared the high cheekbones, slanted eyes, and male beardlessness of their father; and while their mother had taught them the Danish tongue and some of the Danish ways, now it was as merfolk that they talked.

Oldest among them, Tauno took the word. "We must decide where to go. Hard was it to keep death at bay when everyone stayed here. We cannot do it for long alone."

He was likewise the biggest, tall, wide in the shoulders, mightily muscled from a lifetime's swimming. His shoulder-length hair, caught by a beaded headband, was yellow with the least tinge of green; his eyes were amber, set well apart from the blunt nose, above the heavy mouth and jaw; because he had spent much time on the surface or ashore, his hue was brown.

"Why, shall we not follow our father and tribe?" asked Eyjan.

She had nineteen winters. She too was tall, for a woman, and strong with a strength that lay hidden beneath the full curves of breasts, hips, thighs, until she gripped a lover tight or drove a lance into a wallowing walrus. Hers was the whitest skin, for her hair was red, floating out like wings from a challenging gray-eyed young hawk-face.

80

"We know not where they have gone," Tauno reminded her. "It will have to be far, since these were the last good fishing grounds left to our kind around Denmark. And while such merfolk as dwell in the Baltic Sea or along the Norway coast may help them on their way, there is no room for as many more as Liri's people are. The seas are very wide to search, my sister."

"Oh, surely we can ask," Kennin said impatiently. "They'll leave word with someone after they decide." A sparkle jumped in his eyes, making them more than ever summer-blue. "Haa, what a chance to gad about!"

He was of sixteen winters, had yet to fare far, and knew youth's eagerness to be off beyond the horizon. He had not gotten his full growth and would never be tall or broad. On the other hand, he was well-nigh as agile as a merman. His hair was greenish brown, his face round and freckled, his body painted in the loudest-colored patterns the sea dwellers knew. The rest bore no ornament; Tauno was in too bleak a mood, Eyjan had always scoffed at the trouble it cost, and Yria was shy.

That last one whispered: "How can you joke when . . . when . . . everything is gone?"

Her siblings swam closer in around her. To them she was still the babe, left in her crib by a mother whom she was coming more and more to look like. She was small, thin, her breasts only budding; her hair was golden, her eyes huge in the tip-tilted, lip-parted countenance. She had stayed away from revelries as much as a king's daughter might, had never gone off alone with a boy, had spent hours a day learning the womanly arts at which Eyjan jeered—more hours in the dome that had been Agnete's, fondling the treasures that had been Agnete's. Often she lay on the waves, gazing at the green hills and the houses ashore, listening to the bells which called Christian folk to prayer. Of late she had been going there with one or another of her siblings when these would allow, flitting along a twilit strand or behind a wind-gnarled tree or down into the ling like a timid shadow.

Eyjan gave her a quick, rough hug. "You got too big a share of our mortal blood," said the older sister.

Tauno scowled. "And that is a terrible truth," said he. "Yria is not strong. She cannot swim fast, or far without rest and food. What if we are set on by beasts? What if winter catches us away from the warm shallows, or what if the Liri outcasts have moved to Greenland? I do not see how we can take her on any journey."

"Can we not leave her with some foster?" asked Kennin.

Yria shrank into Eyjan's arms. "Oh, no, no," she begged. They could scarcely hear her.

Kennin reddened at his own foolishness. Tauno and Eyjan looked at each other across the hunched and shivering back of their sister. Few were the merfolk who would take in a weakling, when the strong had trouble enough fending for themselves. Now and again one might; but he would do so out of desire. They had no true hope of finding a sea man who would want this child as their father had wanted a certain grown maiden; nor would that be any kindness to the child.

Tauno must gather his will to speak it aloud: "I think, before we leave, we had best take Yria to our mother's people."

4

THE old priest Knud was wakened by a knocking. He climbed from his shut-bed and fumbled a robe on in the dark, for the banked hearthfire gave no real glow; and he felt his way to the door. His bones ached, his teeth clapped with the chill of early spring. He wondered who might be near death. He had outlived every playmate. . . . "I come, in Jesu name, I come."

A full moon was lately risen. It threw a quicksilver bridge on the Kattegat and turned ghostly the hoarfrost on cottage roofs;

but the two crossed streets of Als lay thick with shadow, and the land beyond had become a stalking ground for wolves and trolls. Strangely quiet were the dogs, as if they feared to bark; the whole night was cracklingly still; no, a sound somewhere, hollow, a hoof? The Hell Horse grazing among the graves?

Four stood in a cloud of their own breath. Father Knud gasped and signed himself. He had never seen merfolk, besides the one who had come into his church—unless a glimpse in childhood had been more than a marvelous dream. What else could these be, though? The faces of the tall man and woman were cast in that eldritch mold, the boy's less clearly so, the girl-child's hardly at all. But water dripped and shimmered from her too; she too wore a fishskin tunic and clutched a bone-headed harpoon.

"You, you, you were to have . . . been gone," the priest said, hearing his voice thin in the frozen quiet.

"We are Agnete's children," said the big young man. He spoke Danish with a lilting accent that was indeed, Knud thought wildly, outlandish. "The spell did not touch us."

"No spell—a holy exorcism—" Knud called on God and squared his narrow shoulders. "I pray you, be not wroth with my villagers. The thing was none of their doing or wish."

"I know. We have asked—a friend—about what happened. Be not afraid. Soon we shall go away. First we would give Yria into your care."

The priest was heartened by this, and likewise by seeing that his visitors' bare feet were of human shape and had not left the deep tracks of inhuman weight. He bade the four come in. They did, wrinkling their noses at the grime and smells in the single room which the parish house boasted. He stoked the fire, set forth bread, salt, and beer, and, since they filled the bench, sat down on a stool to talk with them.

Long was that talk. It ended well after he had promised to do his best for the girl. Her three siblings would linger a while to make sure; he must let her go down to the strand every dusk to meet them. Father Knud pleaded with them to stay ashore and be baptized, but this they would not. They kissed their sister and took their leave. She wept, noiselessly and hopelessly, until she fell asleep. The priest tucked her in and got what rest he could on the bench.

Next day, and more and more in the days that followed, Yria was in better spirits. At last she was altogether cheerful. Agnete's kin held aloof, afraid to admit she carried their blood, but Father Knud dealt with her as kindly as his meager means allowed. It helped that she brought gifts of fish and oysters from the sea. To her, the land was as new and wonderful as she was to the children of the hamlet. Erelong she was the middle of a rollicking swarm. As for work, she knew nothing about human tasks but was willing to learn. Maren Pedersdatter tried her on the loom and said she could become uncommonly skillful.

Meanwhile the priest had sent a youth to Viborg, asking what should be done about the girl. Could a halfling be christened? He prayed this be so, for otherwise he knew not what would become of the poor darling. The messenger was gone for a pair of weeks; they must be ransacking their books at the bishopric. Finally he returned, on horse this time, accompanied by guards, a clerical amanuensis, and the provost.

Knud had been giving Christian instruction to Yria, who listened wide-eyed and silent. Now Archdeacon Magnus saw her in the parish house. "Do you truly believe in one God," he barked, "the Father, the Son who is our lord and savior Jesus Christ, and the Holy Ghost which proceeds from them?"

She quailed before his sternness. "I do," she whispered. "I do not understand it very well, but I do believe, good sir."

After further questioning, Magnus told Knud: "There can be no harm in baptizing her. She is not an unreasoning brute, albeit badly in need of more careful teaching before she can be confirmed. If she be devil's bait, the holy water should drive her hence; if she be merely soulless, God will hit upon some way to let us know."

The christening was set for Sunday after mass. The archdeacon gave Yria a white robe to wear and chose a saint's name for her. She grew less afraid of him and agreed to spend the Saturday night in prayer. Friday after sunset, full of eagerness, she wanted her siblings to come to the service—surely the priests would allow it, hoping to win them too—and she cried when they refused.

And so, on a morning of wind, scudding white clouds, dancing glittery waves, before the Als folk in the wooden church, beneath the ship model hung in the nave and Christ hung above the altar, she knelt, and Father Knud led her and the godparents through the rite, and signed her and said with joy, "I baptize you, Margrete, in the name of the Father, and of the Son, and of the Holy Ghost."

She shrieked. Her slight form crumpled. A hissing of breath, some screams and hoarse calls, sounded from the pews. The priest stooped, forgetting his stiffness in his haste, and gathered her to him. "Yria!" he quavered. "What's wrong?"

She looked about her, breathing heavily and with the eyes of one stunned. "I . . . am . . . Margrete," she said. "Who are you?" Provost Magnus loomed over them. "Who are you?"

Knud cast his tear-streaming gaze up toward the archdeacon. "Is it that, that, that she is in truth soulless?" he sobbed.

Magnus pointed to the altar. "Margrete," he said, with such iron in his tone that the whole rough congregation fell silent. "Margrete, look yonder. Who is that?"

Her glance followed the knobbly finger. She raised herself to her knees and drew the cross. "That is our lord and savior Jesus Christ," she said almost steadily.

Magnus lifted his arms. He likewise wept, but for glory. "Lo, a miracle!" he cried. "I thank You, Almighty God, that You have let me, most miserable of sinners, witness this token of Your overflowing grace." He swung on the folk. "Kneel! Praise Him! Praise Him!"

Later, alone with Knud, he explained more calmly: "The bishop and I thought something like this might happen, in particular since your message related the sacred pictures had not turned from her. See you, halflings have indeed no souls, though doubtless their bodies are ageless. Yet God is willing to receive even these. Upon her baptism, He gave her a soul as He gives a soul to a quickening babe. She has become fully human, mortal in the flesh, immortal in the spirit. We must see well to it that she loses not her salvation."

"Why can she not remember?" Knud asked.

"She has been reborn. She keeps the Danish language, with what other human skills she has; but everything that is in any way linked to her former life has been cleansed from her. That must be Heaven's mercy, lest Satan use homesickness to lure the ewe lamb from the fold."

The old man seemed more troubled than pleased. "Her sister and brothers will take this ill."

"I know about them," said Magnus. "Have the girl meet them on the strand in front of those seven low, gnarly trees. Their branches will screen my men, who will have crossbows cocked—"

"No! Never! I will not have it!" Knud gulped, knowing how scant an authority was his. At length he persuaded Magnus not to ambush the halflings. They were leaving soon. And what effect on Margrete's new soul might it have, that almost the first thing she would remember was a deed of blood?

Therefore the priests told the men-at-arms to shoot only if ordered. They waited behind the trees, in a cold, blowing dusk. Margrete's white robe fluttered dimly before them where she stood, puzzled but obedient, hands folded over a rosary.

A sound broke through the soughing of leaves and the clashing of whitecaps. Forth from the water waded the tall man, the tall woman, and the boy. It could just be seen that they were unclad. "Lewdness," Magnus hissed angrily. The man said something in an unknown tongue.

"Who are you?" Margrete replied in Danish. She shrank from them. "I cannot understand you. What do you want?"

"Yria—" The woman held out her wet arms. "Yria." Her own Danish was agonized. "What have they done to you?"

86

"I am Margrete," the girl said. "They told me . . . I must be brave. . . . Who are you? What are you?"

The boy snarled and sprang toward her. She raised the cross. "In Jesu name, begone!" she yelled, horror in her voice. He did not obey, though he stopped when his brother caught him. The tall man made a strangled noise.

Margrete whirled and fled over the dunes toward the hamlet. Her siblings stood a while, talking in tones of bafflement and dismay, before they returned to their sea.

5

INGEBORG Hjalmarsdatter was an Alswoman of about thirty winters. She had been orphaned early and married off to the first younger son who would have her. When she proved barren, and he went down with the boat whereon he worked, leaving her nothing, no other man made an offer. The parish cared for its paupers by binding them over for a year at a time to whoever would take them. Such households knew well how to squeeze out their money's worth in work, without spending unduly on food or clothes for their charges. Ingeborg, instead, got Red Jens to give her passage on his craft to the herring run. She plied what trade she could among the booths on shore, and came back with some shillings. Thereafter she made the trip yearly. Otherwise she stayed home, save when she walked the woodland road to Hadsund for market days.

Father Knud implored her to mend her life. "Can you find me better work than this?" she laughed. He must needs ban her from communion, if not the mass; and she seldom went to the latter, since women hissed her in the streets and might throw a fishhead or a bone at her. The men, easier-going on the whole, did agree she could not be let live among them, if only because of their goodwives' tongues.

She had a cabin built, a shack on the strand a mile north of Als. Most of the unwed young men came to her now and then, and the crews of vessels that stopped in, and the rare chapman, and husbands after dark. Had they no coppers, she would take pay in kind, wherefore she got the name Cod-Ingeborg. Between whiles she was alone, and often strolled far along the shore or into the woods. She had no fear of rovers—they would not likely kill her, and what else mattered?—and little of trolls.

On a winter evening some five years past, when Tauno was just beginning to explore the land, he knocked on her door. After she let him in, he explained who he was. He had been watching from afar, seen men slink in and swagger out; he was trying to learn the ways of his lost mother's folk; would she maybe tell him what this was about? He ended with spending the night. Since, he had many times done so. She was different from the mermaids, warmer somehow in heart as well as flesh; her trade meant naught to him, whose undersea fellows knew no more of marriage than of any other sacrament; he could learn much from her, and tell her much, murmured lip to lip as they lay beneath the coverlet; he liked her for her kindliness and toughness and wry mirth.

For her part, she would take no pay from him, and few gifts. "I do not think ill of most men," she said. "Some, yes, like that cruel old miser Kristoffer into whose hands I would have fallen had I not chosen this way. My skin crawls when he comes smirking." She spat on the clay floor, then sighed. "He has the coin, though. . . . No, mainly they are not bad, those rough-bearded men; and sometimes a lad gives me joy." She rumpled his hair. "You give me more, without fail, Tauno. Can you not see, that is why it would be wrong for you to hire me?"

"No, I cannot," he answered in honesty. "I have things you say men reckon precious, amber, pearls, pieces of gold. If they will help you, why should you not have them?"

"Well," she said, "among other reasons, word would come to

88

the lords around Hadsund, that Cod-Ingeborg was peddling such wares. They would want to know how I got them. I do not wish my last man to wear a hood." She kissed him. "Oh, let us say what is better, that your tales of your undersea wonderland give me more than any hand-graspable wealth may buy."

When Provost Magnus exorcised the merfolk, Ingeborg would see no person for a week. Her eyes were red for a long while afterward.

Thus it stood when Tauno sought her again. He came from the water, naked save for the headband that caught his locks and the sharp flint dagger belted at his hip. In his right hand he carried a trident. It was a chill, misty twilight, fog asmoke until the lap-lapping wavelets were blurred and the early stars were withheld. There was a scent of kelp, fish, and from inland of damp earth and new leaves. The sand gritted beneath his feet, the dune grass scratched his ankles.

A pair of fisher youths were nearing the hut, with a flaring link to show the way. Tauno's Faerie eyes saw further in the dark than men's do. Under the wadmal sameness of hood, smock, and hose, he knew who they were. He trod into their path. "No," he said. "Not this night."

"Why . . . why, Tauno," said one with a foolish grin. "You'd not bar your friends from their bit of fun, would you, or her from this fine big flounder? We won't be long, if you're so eager."

"Go home. Stay there."

"Tauno, you know me, we've talked, played ball, you've come aboard when I was out alone in the jollyboat, I'm Stig—"

"Must I kill you?" asked Tauno without raising his voice.

They looked at him by the guttering link-flare, towering over them, hugely thewed, armed, hair wet as a strandwasher's and faintly green under its fairness, the mer-face and the yellow eyes cold as northlights. They turned and walked hastily back. Through the fog drifted Stig's shout: "They were right about you, you're soulless, you damned *thing*—"

Tauno smote the door of the shack. It was a sagging box of logs weathered gray, peat-roofed, windowless, though light straggled outward and air inward where the chinking moss had fallen. Ingeborg opened for him and closed behind them both. Besides a blubber lamp, she had a low fire going against the chill. Monstrous shadows crawled on the double-width sleeping dais, the stool and table, the few cooking and sewing tools, clothes chest, sausage and stockfish hung from the rafters, and those poles across the rafters which skewered rounds of hardtack. On a night like this, smoke hardly rose from hearthstone to roofhole.

Tauno's lungs always burned for a minute after he had come ashore and emptied them in that single heave which merfolk used. The air was so thin, so dry (and he felt half deafened among its muffled noises, though to be sure he saw better). The reek here was worse. He must cough ere he could speak.

Ingeborg held him, wordlessly. She was short and stocky, snub-nosed, freckled, with a big gentle mouth. Her hair and eyes were dark brown, her voice high but sweet. There have been princesses less well-favored than Cod-Ingeborg. He did not like the smell of old sweat in her gown, any more than he liked any of the stenches of humankind; but underneath it he caught a sunny odor of woman.

"I hoped . . ." she breathed at last. "I hoped. . . ."

He shoved her arms away, stood back, glared and hefted the trident. "Where is my sister?" he snapped.

"Oh. She is, is well, Tauno. None will harm her. None would dare." Ingeborg tried to draw him from the door. "Come, my unhappy dear, sit, have a stoup, be at ease with me."

"First they reaved from her everything that was her life—"

Tauno must stop anew to cough. Ingeborg took the word. "It had to be," she said. "Christian folk could not let her dwell unchristened among them. You can't blame them, Tauno, not even the priests. A higher might than theirs has been in this." She shrugged, with her oft-seen one-sided grin. "For the price of her past, and of growing old, ugly, dead in less than a hundred years, she gains eternity in Paradise. You may live a long while, but when you die you will be done, a blown-out candle flame. Myself, I'll live beyond my body, most likely in Hell. Which of us three is the luckiest?"

Still grim but somewhat calmed, Tauno leaned his fork and sat down on the dais. The straw ticking rustled beneath him. The peat fire sputtered with small blue and yellow dancers; its smoke would have been pleasant if less thick. Shadows crouched in corners and under the roof, and leaped about, misshapen, on the log walls. The cold and dankness did not trouble him, unclad though he was. Ingeborg shivered where she stood.

He peered at her through the murk and smoke. "I know that much," he said. "There is a youth in the hamlet that they hope to make a priest of. So he could tell my sister Eyjan somewhat about it when she found him alone." His chuckle rattled. "She says he is not bad to lie with, save that the open air makes him sneeze." Starkly again: "Well, if that is the way the world swims, naught can we do but give room. However . . . yestre'en Kennin and I went in search of Yria, to make sure she was not being mistreated. Ugh, the mud and filth in those wallows you call streets! Up and down we went, to every house, yes, to church and graveyard. We had not spied her from afar, do you see, not for several days. And we would have known were she inside anything, be it cabin or coffin. She may be mortal now, our little Yria, but her body is still half her father's, and that last night on the strand it had not lost its smell like sunlit waves." Fist thudded on knee. "Kennin and Eyjan raged, would have stormed ashore by full daylight and asked at harpoon point. I told them we would only risk death, and how can the dead help Yria? Yet it was hard to wait till sunset, Ingeborg."

She sat down against him, an arm around his waist, a hand on his thigh, cheek on shoulder. "I know," she said most softly.

He remained unbending. "Well? What has happened, then?"

"Why, the provost took her off with him to Viborg town—Wait! No harm is meant. How could they dare harm a chalice of Heavenly grace?" Ingeborg said that matter-of-factly, and afterward she

91

fleered. "You have come to the right house, Tauno. The provost had a scribe with him, a young cleric, and that one was here and I asked him about any plans for keeping our miracle fed. They are not unkindly in Als, I told him, but neither are they rich; she has no more yarns to spin from undersea; who wants a girl that must be taught afresh like a babe, who wants a foster-daughter to find a dowry for? Oh, she could get something—pauper's work, marriage to a deckhand, or that which I chose—but was this right for a miracle? The cleric said no, nor was it intended. They would bring her back with them and put her in Asmild Cloister at Viborg."

"What is that?" Tauno asked.

Ingeborg did her best to explain. In the end she could say: "They will house Margrete and teach her. When she is of the right age, she will take her vows. Then she will live there in purity, no doubt widely reverenced, until she dies, no doubt in an odor of sanctity. Or do you believe that the corpse of a saint does not stink as yours and mine will?"

Aghast, Tauno exclaimed, "But this is frightful!"

"Oh? Many would count it glorious good fortune."

His eyes stabbed at hers. "Would you?"

"Well . . . no."

"Locked among bleak brick walls for all her days; shorn, harshly clad, ill-fed, droning through her nose at God while letting wither that which God put between her legs; never to know love, children about her, the growth of home and kin, or even wanderings under apple trees in blossom time. . . ."

"Tauno, it is the way to eternal bliss."

"Hm. Rather would I have my bliss now, and then the dark. You too—in your heart—not so?—whether or not you have said you mean to repent on your deathbed. Your Christian Heaven seems to me a shabby place to spend forever."

"Margrete may think otherwise."

"Mar—Aah. Yria." He brooded a while, chin on fist, lips taut, breathing noisily in the smoke. "Well," he said, "if that is what she truly wants, so be it. Yet how can we know? How can *she* know? Will they let her imagine anything is real and right beyond their gloomy cloi . . . cloister? I would not see my little sister cheated, Ingeborg."

"You sent her ashore because you would not see her eaten by eels. Now what choice is there?"

"None?"

The despair of him who had always been strong was like a knife to her. "My dear, my dear." She held him close. But instead of tears, the old fisher hardheadedness rose in her.

"One thing among men opens every road save to Heaven," she said, "and that it does not necessarily bar. Money."

A word in the mer-tongue burst from him. "Go on!" he said in Danish, and clutched her arm with bruising fingers.

"To put it simplest: gold," Ingeborg told him, not trying to break free. "Or that which can be exchanged for gold, though the metal itself is best. See you, if she had a fortune, she could live where she wished—given enough, at the king's court, or in some foreign land richer than Denmark. She would command servants, men-at-arms, warehouses, broad acres. She could take her pick among suitors. Then, if she chose to leave this and return to the nuns, that would be a free choice."

"My father had gold! We can dig it out of the ruins!"

"How much?"

There was more talk. The merfolk had never thought to weigh up what was only a metal to them, too soft for most uses however handsome and unrusting it might be.

At the end, Ingeborg shook her head. "Too little, I fear," she sighed. "In the ordinary course of things, plenty. This is different. Here Asmild Cloister and Viborg Cathedral have a living miracle. She will draw pilgrims from everywhere. The Church is her guardian in law, and will not let her go to a lay family for your few cups and plates."

"What's needed, then?"

"A huge sum. Thousands of marks. See you, some must be

bribed. Others, who cannot be bribed, must be won over by grand gifts to the Church. And then enough must remain that Margrete is a wealthy young lady. . . . Thousands of marks."

"What weight?" Tauno fairly yelled, with an undersea curse.

"I—I—How shall I, fisherman's orphan, who never held one mark at a time in these fingers, how shall I guess? . . . A boatful? Yes, I think a boatload would do."

"A boatload!" Tauno sagged back. He stared before him. "And we have not even a boat."

Ingeborg smiled sadly and ran fingers along his arm. "No man wins every game," she murmured, "nor does any merman. You've done what you could. Let your sister spend threescore years in denying her body, and afterward forever in unfolding her soul. She may remember us, when you are dust and I am burning."

Tauno shook his head. His eyelids squinched together. "No . . . she bears the same blood as I . . . it is not a restful blood . . . she is shy and gentle, but she was born to the freedom of the world's wide seas . . . if holiness curdles in her, during a lifetime among whisker-chinned crones, what of her chances at Heaven?"

"I know not, I know not."

"A freedom of choice, at least. To buy it, a boatload of gold. A couple of wretched tons, to buy Yria's life."

"Tons! Why—I had not thought—Less than that, surely. A few hundred pounds ought to be ample." Eagerness touched Ingeborg. "Do you think you could find that much?"

"Hm . . . wait. Wait. Let me hark back—" Tauno sat bolt upright. "Yes!" he shouted. "I do know!"

"Where? How?"

With the mercury quickness of the sea people, he became a planner. "Long ago was a city of men on an island to the west of these waters," he said, not loud but shiveringly, while he stared into the shadows. "Great it was, and gorged with gold. Its god was a kraken. They cast down weighted offerings to him—treasure, that he cared not about, but with it kine, horses, virgins, and any evildoers they caught: and these the kraken could eat. He need not snatch aught else than a whale now and then—or a ship, to devour its crew, and over the centuries he and his priests had learned the signals which told him that such-and-such vessels were unwanted in Averorn. . . . So the kraken grew sluggish, and appeared not for generations of men; nor was there any need, since the thought lived on elsewhere that no luck would come from attacking Averorn.

"In time the islanders themselves doubted he was more than a fable. Meanwhile a new folk had arisen in the south. Their traders came north, bearing not goods alone, but gods who did not want costly sacrifices. The people of Averorn flocked to these new gods. The temple of the kraken stood empty, its fires grew cold, its priests died and were not replaced. Finally the king of the city ordered an end to the rites at sun-turnings and evennights.

"After one year, dreadful in his hunger, the kraken rose from the sea bottom; and he sank the harbored ships, and his arms reached inland to knock down towers and pluck forth prey; and the waves came after him, the island was whelmed, it foundered and is forgotten by all save the merfolk."

"Why, that is wonderful!" Ingeborg clapped hands together, not thinking of the small children who had gone down with the city. "Oh, I am so glad!"

"It is not that wonderful," Tauno said. "The merfolk remember Averorn because the kraken lairs there yet. We give it a wide berth."

"I . . . I see. You must, however, bear some hope if you—"

"Yes. Worth trying. Look you, woman: Men cannot go undersea. Merfolk have no ships, nor metal weapons that do not soon corrode away. Never have the races worked together. If they did —maybe—"

Ingeborg sat a long time quiet before she said, almost not to be heard, "And maybe you would be slain."

"Yes, yes. What is that? All are born fey. The merfolk stand close—they must—and a single life is of no high account among us. How could I range off to the ends of the world, knowing I had not done what I might for my little sister Yria who looks like our mother?" Tauno gnawed his lip. "The ship, though, and a crew. How to get the ship?"

They talked back and forth, she trying to steer him from his course, he growing more set in it. At last she gave in. "I may be able to show you what you want," she said.

"What? How?"

"You understand the fishing craft of Als are too cockleshell for what you have in mind. Nor could you hire a ship from a respectable owner, you being soulless and your venture being mad. However, there is a cog, not big but still a cog, that works out of Hadsund, the town some miles hence at the end of Mariager Fjord. I go to Hadsund on market days, and thus have come to know her men. She's a cargo tramp, has fared as widely north as Finland, east as Wendland, west as Iceland. In such outlying parts, the crew have not been above a bit of piracy where it looked safe. They're a gang of ruffians, and their skipper the owner is the worst. He came of a good family near Herning, but his father chose the wrong side in the strife between kings' sons, and thus Herr Ranild Espensen has nothing left to him besides this ship. And he swears bitterly at the Hansa, whose fleets are pushing him out of what business he could formerly get.

"It may be he's desperate enough to league with you."

Tauno considered. "Maybe," he said. "Um-m-m . . . we merfolk are not wont to betray and kill our own kind, as men with souls are. I can fight; I would not fear to meet anyone with any weapon or none; still, where it comes to haggling and to being wary of a shipmate, that might be hard for us three siblings."

"I know," Ingeborg said. "Best I go along, to dicker and keep an eye open on your behalf."

He started. "Would you indeed?" After a moment: "You shall have a full share in the booty, dear friend. You too shall be free."

"If we live; otherwise, what matter? But Tauno, Tauno, think not I offer this out of lust for wealth—"

"I must talk with Eyjan and Kennin, of course—we must plan —we must talk further with you—nonetheless—"

"Indeed, Tauno, indeed, indeed. Tomorrow, forever, you shall have what you will from me. Tonight, though, I ask one thing, that you stop this fretting, cast off that byrnie which covers your eyes, and let us be only Tauno and Ingeborg. See, I have drawn off my gown for you."

6

WHEN the black cog *Herning* stood out of Mariager Fjord, she caught a wind that filled her sail and sent her northward at a good clip. On deck, Tauno, Eyjan, and Kennin shed the human clothes—foul, enclosing rags!—that had disguised them during their days of chaffer with Ranild Espensen. A lickerish shout lifted from six of the eight men, at sight of Eyjan white in the sunlight, clad only in tossing coppery-bronze tresses. They were a shaggy, flea-bitten lot, those men, scarred from fights, their leather doublets, wadmal shirts and breeks ripe with old grease stains.

The seventh was a lad of seventeen winters, Nils Jonsen. He had lately come to Hadsund seeking deckhand work to help care for widowed mother and younger siblings, and could get no other berth than this. He was a good-looking boy, slender, flaxen-haired, fresh-faced. His eyes filled with tears. "How beautiful she is," he whispered.

The eighth was the skipper. He scowled and came down off the poopdeck that sheltered the man at the tiller. (There was also a deck over the bows, through which the forepost jutted. Below and between these reached the main deck, with mast, two hatches, tackle, cooking-hearth, and what cargo was carried topside. Among this last were a red granite boulder, three feet through and

97

about a ton in weight; and a dozen extra anchors; and much cable.)

Ranild went to the halflings, where they and Ingeborg stood on the port side watching Jutland's long hills slide by. It was a clear day; the sun cast dazzling glitter across gray-green-blue whitecaps. Wind skirled, rigging thrummed, timbers creaked as the cog's cutwater surged with a bone in its teeth. Overhead, gulls mewed and made a snowstorm of wings. A smell of salt and tar blew around.

"You!" Ranild barked. "God's blood! Make yourselves decent."

Kennin gave him a look of dislike. Those had been hard hours of bargaining, in a back room of an evil inn; and merfolk were not used to a tongue like Ranild's, rougher than a lynx's. "Who are you to speak of decency?" Kennin snapped.

"Ease off," Tauno muttered. He regarded the skipper with no more love but somewhat more coolness. Not tall, Ranild was thick of chest and arm. Black hair, never washed and scanty on top, framed a coarse broken-nosed pale-eyed countenance; snag teeth showed through a beard that spilled halfway down the tub belly. He was dressed like his crew, save that he bore a short sword as well as a knife and floppy boots rather than shoes or bare feet.

"What's the matter?" Tauno asked. "You, Ranild, may like to wear clothes till they rot off you. Why should we?"

"*Herr* Ranild, merman!" The skipper clapped hand on hilt. "My folk were Junkers when yours dwelt among the flatfish—I'm noble yet, Fiend thunder me! It's my ship, I laid out the costs of this faring, you'll by God's bones do what I tell you or swing from the yardarm!"

Eyjan's dagger whipped out, to gleam near his gullet. "Unless we hang you by those louse-nest whiskers," she said.

The sailors reached for knives and belaying pins. Ingeborg pushed between Eyjan and Ranild. "What are we doing?" she cried. "At each other's throats already? You'll not get the gold

98

without the merfolk, Herr Ranild, nor they get it without your help. Hold back, in Jesu name!"

They withdrew a little on either side, still glowering. Ingeborg went on quietly: "I think I know what's wrong. Herr Ranild, these children of the clean sea have been rubbed raw by days in a town where hogs root in the streets, by nights in a room full of stink and bedbugs. Nevertheless, you, Tauno, Eyjan, Kennin, should have listened to a rede well meant if not so well spoken."

"What is that?" Tauno asked.

Ingeborg flushed; her eyes dropped and her fingers wrestled. She said quieter yet: "Remember the agreement. Herr Ranild wanted you, Eyjan, to go below for him and his men. You would not. I said I . . . would do that, and thus we came to terms. Now you are very fair, Eyjan, fairer than any mortal girl can be. It is not right for you to flaunt your loveliness before those who may only look. Our voyage is into deadly danger. We must not let strife arise."

The halfling bit her lip. "I had not thought of that," she owned. Flaring: "But rather than wear those barn-rug rags when we have no need of disguise, I'll kill the crew and we four will man this ship ourselves."

Ranild opened his mouth. Tauno forestalled him: "That's empty talk, sister mine. See here, we can stand the horrible things till we pass Als. There we'll dive down to where Liri was, fetch garments fit to use . . . and cleanse the filth of these off us on the way."

Thus peace was made. Men kept leering at Eyjan, for the rainbow-scaled tunic of three-ply fishskin that she donned showed cleft of breasts and hardly reached past her hips. But they had Ingeborg to take below.

The human clothes were from that woman, who walked alone through rover-haunted woods to Hadsund, got Ranild interested, and met the siblings on the shore of Mariager Fjord. After the bargain was handselled, he had to persuade his men to go along. Gaunt, surly, ash-pale Oluv Ovesen, the second in command, had not hesitated; greed ruled his life. Torben and Lave said they had faced edged steel erenow and looked at the end to face nooses; therefore, why not a kraken? Palle, Tyge, and Sivard had let themselves be talked over. But the last deckhand quit, which was why young Nils Jonsen was taken on.

No one asked Ranild what had become of his former crewman. Secrecy was important, lest priest forbid or noble thrust into the undertaking. Aage was simply never seen again.

That first day the *Herning* passed the broad beaches and thunderous surf of the Skaw, and from the Skagerrak entered the North Sea. She must round Scotland, then work southwest to about a hundred miles beyond Ireland. In spite of being a good sailer, she would need Godsend winds to make it in less than two weeks—which in truth was how long the time became.

Since she was traveling in ballast, there was ample room below decks, and that was where the men slept. The halflings disdained such a gloomy, dirty, rat-scuttering, roach-crawling cave, and took their rest above. They used no bags or blankets, only straw ticks. When the ship was moving slowly, they would dive overboard, frolic about her, maybe vanish beneath the waves for an hour or two.

Ingeborg told Tauno once that she would have liked to stay topside with them; however, Ranild had ordered her to spend the nights in the hold, ready for whoever might want her. Tauno shook his head. "Humans are a nasty lot," he remarked.

"Your sister has become human," she answered. "And have you forgotten your mother, Father Knud, your friends in Als?"

"N-n-no. Nor you, Ingeborg. After we are back home—But of course I will be leaving Denmark."

"Yes." She looked away. "We have another good fellow aboard. The boy Nils."

He was the sole crewman who did not use her, and yet who was always cheerful and polite toward her. (Tauno and Kennin likewise stayed clear of that pallet in the hold; those who now shared her were not honest yeomen and fishers, and for themselves they

100

had waves to tumble in, seal and dolphin to play with, flowing green depths to enter.) Mostly Nils followed Eyjan about with his eyes and, shyly when off watch, himself.

The rest of the crew had no more to do with the halflings than they must. They took the fresh fish brought aboard, but would not speak with the bringers while it was eaten. To Ingeborg they grumbled words like, "Damned heathen . . . uppity . . . talking beasts . . . worse than Jews . . . we'd be forgiven many sins if we cut their throats, wouldn't we? . . . well, before I put my knife in that bare-legged wench, I've something else. . . ." Ranild kept his own counsel. He too stayed aloof from the three after his few tries at friendliness were rebuffed. Tauno had sought to respond; but the skipper's talk bored when it did not disgust him, and he had never learned to dissemble.

He did like Nils. They seldom spoke, though, for Tauno was close-mouthed save when making a poem. Moreover, in age Nils was nearer to Kennin, and those two found a deal of memories and jokes to swap. Among other jobs, hours a day were spent in weaving the extra cable into a great net. Nils and Kennin would sit together at this work, paying no heed to the sullen men around, and laugh and chatter:

"—I swear that was one time an oyster showed surprise!"

"Ha, I mind me of years back when I was a sprat. We kept a few cows, and I was leading one of 'em to a kinsman's bull. By the road was a big gristmill with a waterwheel, and from afar I saw it begin work. A cow has dimmer eyes than a human; this lovesick beast knew only that something large stood in the offing and bellowed. Away she went, me galloping after and yelling till the halter was yanked from my hand. I soon caught her, oh, yes. When she found it was no bull, she stopped, she looked like a blown-up bladder that has been pinpricked, she merely stood until I took the halter, and afterward she shambled along with the meekness of the stunned."

"Ho, ho, let me tell you about when we boys dressed a walrus in my father's robe of state—"

Eyjan would often join in as merrily. She did not follow ladylike ways, even in the slight degree that mermaids did. She haggled her red locks off at the shoulders, wore no ring or necklace or golden gown save at festivals, would rather hunt whales and challenge the breakneck surf around a skerry than sit tame at home. For the most part she scorned the landfolk (in spite of which, she had prowled the woods with cries of delight for blossoms, birdsong, deer, squirrel, autumn's fiery leaves and the snow and icicles that glittered after). But of some she was fond, Nils among them. Also, she did not lie with her brothers—the one Christian law which Agnete had gotten well into her children—and the mermen were gone to an unknown place and the lads of Als were far behind.

The *Herning* plowed through day and night, squall and calm, until she raised what Tauno and Ranild agreed were the southern Orkney islands. That was toward evening: mild weather, fair wind, light summer night and a full moon due up. They saw no reason not to push on through the narrows after sunset, the more so when the brothers offered to swim ahead as waterline lookouts. Eyjan wanted to do the same, but Tauno said one must stay back against possible disaster like a sudden onslaught by sharks; and when they drew lots, hers was the short straw. She cursed for a quarter hour without repeating herself before she calmed down.

Thus it happened that she stood alone on the main deck, near the forecastle. Another lookout was perched aloft, screened from her by the bellying sail, and a helmsman was under the poop, hidden in its shadow. The rest, who had learned to trust the halflings in watery matters, snored below.

Save for Nils, who came back and found Eyjan there. The moonlight sparkled on her tunic, sheened on her face and breast and limbs, lost itself in her hair. It washed the deck clean, it built a shivering road from the horizon to the laciness of foam on small waves. They slapped very gently on the hull, those waves, and Nils, who was barefoot, could feel it, because the ship was heeled just enough that he became aware of standing. The sail, dull brown with leather crisscrossing by day, stood overhead like a snowpeak. The rigging creaked, the wind lulled, the sea murmured. It was almost warm. Far, far above, in a dreamy half darkness, glinted stars.

"Good evening," he said awkwardly.

She smiled at the tall, frightened boy. "Welcome," she said.

"Have you . . . may I . . . may I join you?"

"I wish you would." Eyjan pointed to where the light picked out a couple of widely spaced roils on the port and starboard quarters. "I long to be with them. Take my mind off it, Nils."

"You, you, you do love your sea, no?"

"What better thing to love? Tauno made a poem once—I cannot put it well into Danish—let me try: *Above, she dances, clad in sun, in moon, in rain, in wind, strewing gulls and spindrift kisses. Below, she is green and gold, calm, all-caressing, she whose children are reckoned by shoals and herds and pods and flocks beyond knowing, giver and shelterer of the world. But farthest down she keeps what she will not ever let the light see, mystery and terror, the womb wherein she bears herself. Maiden, Mother, and Mistress of Mysteries, enfold at the end my weary bones! . . . No.*" Eyjan shook her head. "That is not right. Maybe if you thought of your earth, the great wheel of its year, and that . . . Mary? . . . who wears a cloak colored like the sky, maybe then you could—I know not what I am trying to say."

"I cannot believe you are soulless!" Nils cried softly.

Eyjan shrugged. Her mood had shifted. "They tell me our kind was friendly with the old gods, and with older gods before them. Yet never have we made offering or worship. I've tried and failed to understand such things. Does a god need flesh or gold? Does it matter to him how you live? Does it swerve him if you grovel and whimper? Does he care whether you care about him?"

"I cannot bear to think you will someday be nothing. I beg you, get christened."

"Ho! Likelier would you come undersea. Not that I could bring you myself. My father knows the spells for that; we three don't."

103

She laid a hand over his, where he gripped the rail till his fingers hurt. "Yet I would fain take you, Nils," she said low. "Only for a while, only to share what I love with you."

"You are too . . . too kind." He started to go. She drew him back.

"Come," she smiled. "Under the foredeck are darkness and my bed."

Tauno and Kennin did not swim watch for nothing. They warned of a reef, and later of a drifting boat, perhaps broken loose from a ship that was towing it. These were trafficked waters this time of year. Ranild felt cordial toward the brothers when they came aboard at dawn.

"God's stones!" he bawled, laying hand on Kennin's shoulder. "Your breed could turn a pretty penny in royal fleet or Hansa."

The boy slipped free. "I fear the penny must be prettier than they can afford," he laughed, "to make me stand in an outhouse breath like yours."

Ranild cuffed after him. Tauno stepped between. "No more," the oldest halfling rapped. "We know what work is to be done and how the gains are to be shared. Best not overtread—from either side."

Ranild stamped from them with a spit and a curse. His men growled.

Soon afterward Nils found himself circled by four off watch, up on the poop. They cackled and nudged him, and when he would not answer them they drew knives and spoke of cutting him till he did. Later they were to say it was not really meant. But that was then. At the time, Nils broke through, tumbled down the ladder and ran forward.

The halflings lay asleep beneath the forecastle. It was a blue day of blithe winds; a couple of sails were on the horizon, gull wings betokened the nearness of land.

The merman's children woke with animal quickness. "What's wrong now?" asked Eyjan, placing herself beside the youth. She drew the steel dagger that, like her brothers, she had gotten Ingeborg to buy for her with a bit of Liri gold. Tauno and Kennin flanked them, harpoons in hand.

"They—oh—they—" Red and white flew over Nils' cheeks. The tongue locked in his mouth.

Oluv Ovesen shambled ahead of leering Torben, Palle, and Tyge. (Ranild and Ingeborg slept below; Lave was at the helm, Sivard on lookout in the crow's nest; these last watched with drool and catcalls.) The mate kept blinking his white lashes and peeling lips back from his buck teeth. "Well, well," he hailed, "who's next, mermaid?"

Eyjan's eyes were flint gray, storm gray. "What mean you," she answered, "if ever a yapping cur means anything?"

Oluv stopped two ells short of those threatening spears. Angrily, he said: "Tyge was at the tiller last night and Torben at the masthead. They saw you go beneath the foredeck with this milksop boy. They heard you two whispering, thrashing, thumping, and moaning."

"And what has my sister to do with you?" Kennin bristled.

Oluv wagged a finger. "This," he said: "that we went along as honest men with leaving her alone; but if she spreads her legs for one, she does for all."

"Why?"

"Why? Because we're all in this together, you. And anyway, what right has a sea cow to give herself airs and pick and choose?" Oluv sniggered. "Me first, Eyjan. You'll have more fun with a real man, I promise you."

"Go away," said the girl, shaking with fury.

"There's three of them," Oluv said to his crewfolk. "I don't count little Nils. Lave, lash the tiller. Hallohoi, Sivard, come on down!"

"What do you intend?" Tauno asked in a level voice.

Oluv picked his teeth with a fingernail. "Oh, nothing much, fishman. I think best we hogtie you and your brother for a while. Nothing worse, if you behave yourselves. Your sister'll soon be thanking us."

Eyjan yelled like a cat. Kennin snarled, "I'll see you in the Black Ooze first!" Nils groaned, tears breaking loose; one hand drew his knife, the other reached for Eyjan. Tauno waved them back. His mer-face was quite moveless within the wind-blown locks.

"Is this your unbreakable will?" he asked tonelessly.

"It is," Oluv told him.

"I see."

"You, she . . . soulless . . . two-legged beasts. Beasts have no rights."

"Oh, but they do. However, turds do not. Enjoy yourself, Oluv." And Tauno launched his harpoon.

The mate screamed when those barbs entered his guts. He fell and lay flopping on the deck, spouting blood, yammering and yammering. Tauno leaped to snatch the now loosened shaft. Wielding it like a quarterstaff, he waded into the crewmen. His siblings and Nils came behind. "Don't kill them!" Tauno roared. "We need their hands!"

Nils got no chance to fight. His comrades were too swift. Kennin drove stiffened fingers into Torben's midriff and, wheeling, kneed Palle in the groin. Tauno's shaft laid Tyge flat. Eyjan bounded to meet Lave, who was running at her from aft; she stopped when they had almost met, caught his body on her hip, and sent him flying to crack his head against the foredeck ladder. Sivard scrambled back aloft. And that was that.

Ranild came howling from the hold. Confronted by three halflings and a strong lad, he must needs agree, no matter how sulkily, that Oluv Ovesen had fallen on his own deeds. Ingeborg helped by reminding everyone that this meant fewer to share the booty. A kind of truce was patched together, and Oluv's corpse sent overside with a rock from the ballast lashed to the ankles so he would not bring bad luck by rising to look at his shipmates.

Thereafter Ranild and his men spoke no unnecessary word to the merman's children—or to Nils, who slept with the latter lest he get a knife in the kidneys. Given such close quarters, the boy

106

could do nothing to Eyjan save adore her. She would smile and pat his cheek, but absently; her mind was elsewhere.

Ingeborg sought out Tauno in the bows and warned him that the crew did not mean for those they hated to live many days past the time the gold was aboard. She got them to talk by herself pretending loathing for the merfolk, claiming to have befriended these in the same spirit as one might trick an ermine into a trap for its pelt.

"Your word is no surprise," Tauno said. "We'll stand watch and watch, the whole way home." He looked at her. "How haggard you've grown!"

"Easier was it among the fishermen," she sighed.

He took her chin in his hand. "When we get back, if we do," he said, "you will have the freedom of the world. If we do not, you will have peace."

"Or Hell," she said tiredly. "I did not come along either for freedom or for peace. Now best we stay apart, Tauno, so they won't think we are of the same heart."

What kept Eyjan busy, and Tauno and Kennin, was the search for lost Averorn. Merfolk always knew where they were; but the halflings did not know where their goal was, within two or three hundred miles. They swam out to ask of passing dolphins—not in just that way, for beasts do not use language of the human kind, yet merfolk had means for getting help from creatures they believed to be their cousins.

And directions were indeed gotten, more and more exact as the ship drew nearer. Yes, a bad place, said Flipperdipper, a kraken lair, ah, steer clear . . . it is true that krakens, like other cold-blooded beings, can lie long unfed; however, this one must be ravenous after centuries with naught but stray whales . . . he stays there, said Sheerfin, because he still thinks it is his Averorn, he broods on its drowned treasures and towers and the bones that once worshipped him . . . he has grown, I hear tell, until his arms reach from end to end of the ruined main square . . . well, for old times' sake we'll guide you thither, said Spraybow, seeing as how the moon wanes toward the half, which is when he goes to sleep, though he is readily aroused . . . but no, give you more than guidance, no, we have too many darlings to think about. . . .

In this wise did the *Herning* at last reach that place in the ocean beneath which lay sunken Averorn.

7

THE dolphins took hasty leave. Their finned gray backs were rainbowed by the morning sun, in mist off the froth cast up by their flukes. Tauno felt sure they would go no further than to the nearest edge of safety; that was an unslakably curious and gossipy breed.

He had laid a course to bring the cog here at this time, giving a full day's light for work. Now the sail was furled and the broadbeamed hull hardly rocked at rest. For it was a calm day, with the least of breezes in an almost cloudless heaven. Waves went small and chuckling, scant foam aswirl on their tops. Looking overside, Tauno marveled as he had done throughout his life, how intricately and beautifully wrinkled each wave was, no two alike, no one ever the same as its past self. And how warmly the sunlight spilled over his skin, how coolly the salt air blessed him! He had not broken his fast, that being an unwise thing to do before battle, and was aware of his belly, and this too was good, like every awareness.

"Well," he said, "soonest begun, soonest done."

The sailors goggled at him. They had broken out pikes, which they clutched as if they were trying to keep afloat on them. Behind suntan, dirt, and hair, five of those faces were terrified; Adam's apples bobbed in gullets. Ranild stood stoutly, a crossbow cocked on his left arm. And while Nils was pale, he burned and shivered

108

with the eagerness of a lad too young to really know that young lads can also die.

"Get busy, you lubbers," jeered Kennin. "We're doing the work that counts. Can't you turn a windlass?"

"I give the orders, boy," said Ranild with unwonted calm. "Still, he's right. Hop to it."

Sivard wet his lips. "Skipper," he said hoarsely, "I . . . I think best we put about."

"After coming this far?" Ranild grinned. "Had I known you're a woman, I could have gotten some use out of you."

"What's gold to an eaten man? Shipmates, think! The kraken can haul us undersea the way we haul up a hooked flounder. We—"

Sivard spoke no more. Ranild decked him with a blow that brought nosebleed. "Man the tackle, you whoresons," the owner rasped, "or Satan fart me out if I don't send you to the kraken myself!"

They scurried to obey. "He does not lack courage," Eyjan said in the mer-tongue.

"Nor does he lack treachery," Tauno warned. "Turn never your back on any of that scurvy lot."

"Save Nils and Ingeborg," she said.

"Oh, you'd not want to turn your *back* on him, or I on her," Kennin laughed. He likewise felt no fear, he was wild to be off.

Using a crane they had fitted together, the sailors raised that which had been readied on the way. A large piece of iron had been hammered into the boulder till it stood fast; thereafter the outthrusting half was ground and whetted to a barbed spearhead. Elsewhere in the rock were rings, and the huge net was secured to these at its middle. Along the outer edges of the net were tied the twelve ship-anchors. All this made a sort of bundle lashed to a raft whose right size had been learned by trial and error. The crane arm dangled it over the starboard bulwark, tilting the cog.

"Let's go," said Tauno. He himself was unafraid, though at the back of his head he did think on the fact that this world—that entered him and that he entered through senses triply heightened by danger—might soon crack to an end, not only in its present and future but in its very past.

The siblings took off their clothes, save for headbands and dagger belts. Each slung a pair of harpoons across the back. They stood for a moment at the rail, their sea ablaze behind them, tall Tauno, lithe Kennin, Eyjan of the white skin and the comely breasts.

To them came Nils. He wrung their hands, he kissed the girl, he wept because he could not go with them. Meanwhile Ingeborg held hands and eyes with Tauno. She had braided her hair, but a stray brown lock fluttered across her brow. Upon her snub-nosed, wide-mouthed, freckled face had come a grave loveliness he had never known before, not ever among the merfolk.

"It may be I will not see you again, Tauno," she said, too low for others to listen, "and sure it is that I cannot and must not speak what is in my heart. Yet I will pray for this, that if you go to your death, on your errand for a sister's sake, God give you in your last moment the pure soul you have earned."

"Oh . . . you are kind, but—Well, I fully mean to come back."

"I drew a bucket of sea water ere dawn," she whispered, "and washed myself clean. Will you kiss me farewell?"

He did. "Overboard!" he shouted, and plunged.

Six feet beneath, the sea took him with a joyful splash. It sheathed him in aliveness. He savored the taste and coolth for a whole minute before he called, "Lower away."

The sailors cranked down the laden raft. It floated awash, weight exactly upheld. Tauno cast it loose. The humans crowded to the rail. The halflings waved—not to them but to wind and sun—and went under.

The first breath of sea was always easier than the first of air. One simply blew out, then stretched wide the lips and chest. Water came in, tingling through mouth, nostrils, throat, lungs, stomach, guts, blood, to the farthest hair and nail. That dear shock threw the body over to merfolk way: subtle humors decomposed the fluid element itself to get the stuff which sustains fish, fowl, flesh, and fire alike;

salt was sieved from the tissues; interior furnaces stoked themselves high against the lamprey chill.

That was a reason why merfolk were scarce. They required more food afloat than men do ashore. A bad catch or a murrain among the whales might make an entire tribe starve to death. The sea gives; the sea takes.

Agnete's children placed themselves to manhandle their clumsy load and swam downward.

At first the light was like new leaves and old amber. Soon it grew murky, soon afterward blackness ate the last of it. No matter their state, the siblings felt cold. Silence hemmed them in. They were headed for depths below any in Kattegat or Baltic; this was the Ocean.

"Hold," Tauno said, in the mer-tongue that was meant to be spoken underwater, a language of many hums, clicks, and smacks. "Is she riding steady? Can you keep her here?"

"Aye," answered Eyjan and Kennin.

"Good. Let this be where you wait."

They made no bold protests. They had worked out their plan and now abode by it, as those must who dare the great deep. Tauno, strongest and most skilled, was to scout ahead.

Strapped on the left forearm, each of them carried a lantern from Liri. This was a hollowed crystal globe, plated with varnished silver on one half and shaped into lenses on the other half, filled with that living seafire which lit the homes of the merfolk. A hole, covered with mesh too fine for those tiny animals to escape, let them be fed and let water go in and out. The ball rested in a box of carven bone, shuttered in front. None of the lanterns had been opened.

"Fare you lucky," said Eyjan. The three embraced in the dark. Tauno plunged.

Down he swam and down. He had not thought his world could grow blacker, bleaker, stiller, but it did. Again and yet again he worked muscles in chest and belly to help inside pressure become the same as outside. Nevertheless it was as if the weight of every foot he sank were loaded on him.

111

At last he felt, as a man at night may feel a wall in front of him, that he neared bottom. And he caught an odor . . . a taste . . . a sense . . . of rank flesh; and through the water pulsed the slow in-and-out of the kraken's gills.

He uncovered the lantern. Its beam was pale and did not straggle far; but it served his Faerie eyes. Awe crawled along his backbone.

Below him reached acres of ruin. Averorn had been large, and built throughout of stone. Most had toppled to formless masses in the silt. But here stood a tower, like a last snag tooth in a dead man's jaw; there a temple only partly fallen, gracious colonnades around a god who sat behind his altar and stared blind into eternity; yonder the mighty wreck of a castle, its battlements patrolled by weirdly glowing fish; that way the harbor, marked off by mounds that were buried piers and city walls, still crowded with galleons; this way a house, roof gone to show the skeleton of a man forever trying to shield the skeletons of a woman and child; and every-where, everywhere burst-open vaults and warehouses, the upward twinkle of gold and diamonds on the seabed!

And sprawled at the middle was the kraken. Eight of his darkly gleaming arms reached into the corners of the eight-sided plaza that bore his mosaic image. His remaining two arms, the longest, twice the length of the *Herning*, were curled around a pillar at the north side which bore on top the triskeled disc of that god he had conquered. His terrible finned head sagged loosely over them; Tauno could just glimpse the hook beak and a swart lidless eye.

The halfling snapped back the shutter and started to rise in light-lessness. A throbbing went through the ocean, into his bones. It was as if the world trembled. He cast a beam downward. The kra-ken was stirring. He had awakened him.

Tauno clenched his teeth. Wildly he dug hands and feet into that chill thick water; he ignored the pain of pressure too hastily lifted; yet icily with merfolk senses he noted which way he moved. It rumbled below him. The kraken had stretched and gaped, a portico had been knocked to pieces.

112

At the verge of daylight, Tauno halted. He hung afloat and blinked with his lantern. A vast shadowiness swelled beneath.

Now, till Kennin and Eyjan got here, he must stay alive—yes, hold the kraken in play so it would not go elsewhere.

In the middle of that rising stormcloud body, he saw a baleful gleam of eyes. The beak clapped. An arm coiled out at him. Upon it were suckers that could strip his ribs. Barely did he swerve aside from its snatching. It came back, loop after loop of it. He drove his knife in to the hilt. The blood which smoked forth when he withdrew the blade tasted like strong vinegar. The arm struck him and he rolled off end over end, in pain and his head awhirl.

Another arm and another closed in. He wondered dazedly who he was to fight a god. Somehow he unslung a harpoon. Before the crushing grip had him, he swam downward with all his speed. Maybe he could get a stab in that mouth.

A shattering scream blasted him into darkness.

He came to a minute later. His head ached, his ears tolled. Around him the water had gone wild. Eyjan and Kennin were at his sides, upholding him. He glanced blurrily bottomward and saw a shrinking inkiness. The kraken hooted and threshed as it sank.

"Look, oh, look!" Kennin jubilated. He pointed with his own lantern. Through blood, sepia, and seething, the wan ray picked out the kraken in his torment.

Brother and sister had towed their weapon above him. They had cut it free of its raft. The spear, with a ton of rock behind it, had pierced the body of the kraken.

"Are you hurt?" Eyjan asked Tauno. Her voice wavered through the uproar around. "Can you get about?"

"I'd better be able to," he mumbled. Shaking his head seemed to clear away some of the fog.

The kraken sank back into the city he had murdered. The spear wound, while grievous, had not ended his cold life, nor was the weight of the boulder more than he could lift. However, around him was the outsize net.

113

And now the merman's children came to grab the anchors on the rim of that net and make them fast in the ruins of Averorn.

Desperate was their work, with the giant body threshing, the giant arms flailing and clutching. Cast-up ooze and vomited ink blinded eyes, choked lungs, in stinking clouds; cables whipped, tangled, and snapped; walls broke under blows that sent doomsday thunders through the water; the hootings beat on skulls and clawed at eardrums; the attackers were hit, cast bruisingly aside, scraped by barnacled skin until their own blood added iron taste to the acid of the kraken's; they were a battered three who finally pegged the monster down.

But bind it they did. And they swam to where its huge head throbbed and threshed, its beak snapped at the imprisoning strands, its arms squirmed like a snakepit under the mesh. Through the murk-mists they looked into those wide, awarenessful eyes. The kraken had stopped his clamor. They heard only a rush of current, in and out of his gills. He glared unflinchingly at them.

"Brave have you been," said Tauno, "a fellow dweller in the sea. Therefore know that you are not being killed for gain."

He took the right eye, Kennin the left. They thrust their harpoons in to the shaft ends. When that did not halt the strugglings, they used their second pair, and both of Eyjan's. Kraken blood and kraken anguish drove them off.

After a while it was over. Some of their weapons must have worked into the brain and slashed it.

The siblings fled from Averorn to the sunlight. They sprang into air and saw the cog wallowing in heavy seas that the fight in the deeps had raised. Tauno and Eyjan did not bother to unload their lungs, though air-breathing they would be lighter than water. They kept afloat with gentle paddling, let the ocean soothe and croon to their aching bodies, and drank draught upon draught of being alive. It was young Kennin who shouted to those clustered white-faced at the bulwarks: "We did it! We slew the kraken! The treasure is ours!"

At that, Nils ran up the ratlines crowing like a cock and Ingeborg burst into tears. The other sailors gave a cheer that was oddly short; thereafter they kept eyes mainly on Ranild.

Through the waves leaped the dolphins, two score of them, to hear the tale.

Work remained. Ranild cast the swimmers a long weighted line with a sack and a hook at the end. They took it back under.

Already the glow-fish he had been too slow to catch were nibbling on the kraken. "Let's do our task and be away from here as fast as we can," said Tauno. His followers agreed. They liked not poking around a tomb.

Yet for Margrete who had been Yria they did. Over and over they filled the bag with coin, plate, rings, crowns, ingots; over and over they hung on the hook a golden chest or horn or candelabrum or god. A signal would not travel well along this length of rope; the crew simply hauled it in about every half hour. Tauno discovered he had better attach his lantern, for, although the sea above had quieted, the *Herning* did drift around and the line never descended to the same place. Between times the merman's children searched for new hoards, or rested, or fed themselves off the cheese and stockfish Ingeborg had laid in the sack.

Until Tauno said wearily: "We were told several hundred pounds would be ample, and I swear we've lifted a ton. A greedy man is an unlucky man. Shall we begone?"

"Oh, yes, oh, yes." Eyjan peered into the glooms that bulked around their sphere of weak light. She shivered and huddled close to her elder brother. Rarely before had he seen her daunted.

Kennin was not. "I begin to know why the landfolk are so fond of looting," he said with a grin. "There's fun in an endlessness of baubles as in an endlessness of ale or women."

"Not truly endless," Tauno answered in his sober fashion.

"Why, is it not endlessness if you have more of something than you can finish off in your lifetime, gold to spend, ale to drink, women—?" Kennin laughed.

"Bear with him," Eyjan said into Tauno's ear. "He's a boy. All creation is opening for him."

115

"I'm no oldster myself," Tauno replied, "though the trolls know I feel like one."

They rid themselves of the remaining lanterns, putting these in the last bagful. It would rise faster than was wise for them. Tauno gestured salute to unseen Averorn. "Sleep well," he murmured; "may your rest be unbroken till the Weird of the World."

From cold, dark, and death, they passed into light and thence into air. The sun cast nearly level beams out of the west, whose sky was greenish; eastward, amidst royal blue, stood forth the evening star. Waves ran purple and black, filigreed with foam, though the breeze had stopped. Their rush and squelp were the sole sounds in that coolness, except for what was made by the lolloping dolphins.

These wanted at once to know everything, but the siblings were too tired. They promised full news tomorrow, coughed the water from their lungs, and made for the cog. None waited at the rail save Herr Ranild. A rope ladder dangled down amidships.

Tauno came first aboard. He stood dripping, shivering a bit, and looked around. Ranild bore crossbow in crook of arm; his men gripped their pikes near the mast—The kraken was dead! Why this tautness among them? Where were Ingeborg and Nils?

"Um-m-m . . . you're satisfied?" Ranild rumbled in his whiskers.

"We have plenty for my sister, and to make the lot of you rich," Tauno said. His muscles dragged at him, chilled, bruised, worn out. The same ache and dullness were in his head. He felt he ought to be chanting his victory; no, that could wait, let him only rest now, only sleep.

Eyjan climbed over the bulwark. "Nils?" she called.

A look across the six who stood there sent the knife hissing from her scabbard. "Treachery—this soon?"

"Kill them!" Ranild shouted.

Kennin had just come off the ladder. He was still poised on the rail. As the sailors and their pikes surged forward, he yelled and pounced to the deck. None among those clumsy shafts had swift-

116

ness to halt him. Straight at Ranild's throat he flew, blade burning in the sunset glow.

Ranild lifted the crossbow and fired. Kennin crashed at his feet. The quarrel had gone through breastbone, heart, and back. Blood poured across the deck.

It stabbed in Tauno: Ingeborg had warned of betrayal, but Ranild was too shrewd for her. He must have plotted with man after single man, in secret corners of the hold. The moment the swimmers went after their booty, he gave the word to seize the woman and Nils. And slay them? No; that might leave traces; bind them, gag them, lay them below decks, until the trusting halflings had returned.

Eyjan's quick understanding, Kennin's ready action had upset the plan. The onrush of the sailors was shaken and slowed. There was time for Eyjan and Tauno to dive overboard.

A couple of pikes arced harmlessly after them. Ranild loomed at the rail, black across the evening. His guffaw boomed forth: "Maybe this'll buy your passage home from the sharks!" And down to them he cast the body of Kennin.

8

THE dolphins gathered.

With them, after the manner of merfolk, Tauno and Eyjan left their brother. They had closed the eyes, folded the hands, and taken the knife—steel beginning to rust—that it might go on in use as something that had known him. Now it was right that he should make the last gift which was his to give, not to the conger eels but to those who had been his friends.

The halflings withdrew a ways while the long blue-gray shapes surrounded Kennin—very quietly, very gently—and they sang across the sunset ocean that farewell which ends:

> *"Wide shall you wander, at one with the world,*
> *Ever the all of you eagerly errant:*
> *Spirit in sunlight and spindrift and sea-surge,*
> *Flesh in the fleetness of fish and of fowl,*
> *Back to the Bearer your bone and your blood-salt.*
> *Beloved:*
> *The sky take you.*
> *The sea take you.*
> *And we will remember you in the wind."*

"But oh, Tauno, Tauno!" Eyjan wept. "He was so young!"

Her brother held her close. The low waves rocked them. "Stark are the Norns," Tauno said. "He made a good ending."

A dolphin came to them and asked in dolphin wise what more help they wished. It would not be hard to keep the ship hereabouts, as by smashing its rudder. Presently thirst would wreak justice.

Tauno glanced at the cog, becalmed on the horizon, sail furled. "No," he said, "they hold hostages. Nevertheless, something must be done."

"I'll cut open Herr Ranild's belly," Eyjan said, "and tie the end of his gut to the mast, and chase him around the mast till he's lashed to it."

"I hardly think him worth that much trouble," Tauno said. "Dangerous is he, though. To attack the ship herself, with the dolphins or by swimming beneath and prying plank from plank, is no trick. To seize it, on the other hand, may be impossible. Yet must we try, for Yria, Ingeborg, and Nils. Come, we'd better take food—our cousins will catch us some—and rest. Our strength has been spent."

A while after midnight he awoke refreshed. Grief had not drained from him; however, the keenness for rescue and revenge filled most of his being.

Eyjan slept on, awash in a cloud of her hair. Strange how innocent, almost childlike her face had become, lips half parted and long lashes down over cheekbones. Around her were the guardian dolphins. Tauno kissed her in the hollow where throat met breast, and swam softly away.

It was a light night of Northern summer. Overhead, heaven stood aglow, a twilight wherein the stars looked small and tender. The waters glimmered, barely moving, a lap-lap-lap of wavelets above the deeper half-heard march of the tide. The air was hushed, cool, and damp.

Tauno came to the *Herning*. He circled it with the stealthiness of a shark. Nobody seemed to be at the helm, but a man stood at either rail, pike agleam, and a third was in the crow's nest. The riding lights were left dark so as not to dazzle their eyes. That meant three below. They were standing watch and watch. Ranild was taking no chances with his foes.

Or was he? The rail amidships lay a mere six feet above the water. One might find means to climb—

And maybe kill a man or two before the racket fetched everybody else. Useless, that. The merman's children had beaten the whole crew erenow; but that had been when no sailor carried more than a knife, and none really looked for a battle, and anyhow—once Oluv the White was out of the way—it had been no death-fight.

And Kennin was gone.

With naught save his face reaching from the water, Tauno waited for what might happen.

At length he heard a footfall, and the man who blotted the starboard sky called, "Well, well, do you pant for us already?"

"You're on watch, remember," came Ingeborg's voice—how dragging, how utterly empty! "I could grit my teeth and seduce you if I thought the skipper would hang you for leaving your post; but no such luck. No, I left that sty in the hold for a breath of air, forgetting that here also are horrible swine."

"Have a care, slut. You know we can't risk leaving you alive for a witness, but there are ways and ways to die."

"And if you get too saucy, we may not keep you till the last night out," said the man on the port side. "That gold'll buy me more whores than I can handle, so why bother with Cod-Ingeborg?"

"Yes, piss on her," said the man aloft, and tried to. She fled weeping under the poop. Laughter bayed at her heels.

Tauno stiffened for a minute. Then, ducking silently below, he made his way to the rudder.

Its barnacles were rough and its weeds were slimy in his grasp. He lifted himself with more slowness and care than he had used in scouting the kraken's den. Because of sheer the tiller was about eight feet overhead, in that cavern made by the upper deck. Tauno caught the post with both hands, curved his body, and got toes in between post and hull, resting on a bracket. In a smooth motion, not stopping to wince as the bronze dug into his flesh, he rose to where he could crook fingers on the after rail; and thus he chinned himself up.

"What was that?" cried a sailor on the twilit main deck.

Tauno waited. The water dripped off him no louder than wavelets patted the hull. It felt cold.

"Ah, a damned dolphin or something," said another man. "Beard of Christ, I'll be glad to leave these creepy waters!"

"What's the second thing you'll do ashore?" A coarse three-way gabbing began. Tauno reached Ingeborg. She had drawn one breath when she saw him athwart silvery-dark heaven. Afterward she stood most quiet, save for the wild flutterings of her heart.

He caught her to him in the lightlessness under the poop. Even then he marked the rounded firmness of her, the warm fragrance, the hair that tickled his lips laid close to her ear. But he whispered merely: "How goes it on board? Is Nils alive?"

"Until tomorrow." She could not reply with quite the steadiness that Eyjan would have shown; but she did well. "They tied and gagged us both, you know. Me they'll keep a while—did you hear? They're not so vile that Nils has any use for them. He lies bound, of course. They talked about what to do with him while he listened. Finally they decided the best sport would be to watch him sprattle from the yardarm tomorrow morning." Her nails dug into his arm.

120

"Were I not a Christian woman, how good to spring overboard into your sea!"

He missed her meaning. "Don't. I couldn't help you; if naught else, you'd die of chill. . . . Let me think, let me think. . . . Ah."

"What?" He could hear how she warned herself not to hope.

"Can you pass a word to Nils?"

"Maybe when he's hailed forth. They'll surely make me come along."

"Well . . . if you can without being overheard, tell him to lift his heart and be ready to fight." Tauno pondered a minute. "We need to pull eyes away from the water. When they're about to put the rope around Nils' neck, let him struggle as much as he's able. And you too: rush in, scratch, bite, kick, scream."

"Do you think—do you believe—really—Anything, I'll do anything. God is merciful, that He . . . He lets me die in battle at your side, Tauno."

"Not that! Don't risk yourself. If a knife is drawn at you, yield, beg to be spared. And take shelter from the fighting. I don't need your corpse, Ingeborg, I need you."

"Tauno, Tauno." Her mouth sought his.

"I must go," he breathed in her ear. "Until tomorrow."

He went back to the sea as cautiously as he had left it. Because his embrace had wet her ragged gown, Ingeborg thought best to stay where she was while it dried. She wouldn't be getting to sleep anyway. She fell on her knees. "Glory to God in the highest," she stammered. "Hail, Mary, full of grace—oh, you're a woman, you'll understand—the Lord is with you—"

"Hey, in there!" a sailor shouted. "Stow that jabber! Think you're a nun?"

"How'd you like me for a divine bridegroom?" called the mast-head lookout.

Ingeborg's voice fell silent; her soul did not. And erelong the watchers' heed went elsewhere. Dolphins came to the ship, a couple of dozen, and circled and circled. In the pale night their wake boiled after them, eerily quiet; their backfins stood forth like sharp

121

weapons; the beaks grinned, the little eyes rolled with a wicked mirth.

The men called Ranild from his bunk. He scowled and tugged his beard. "I like this not," he mumbled. "Cock of Peter, how I wish we'd skewered those last two fishfolk! They plot evil, be sure of that. . . . Well, I doubt they'll sink the cog, for how then shall they carry the gold? Not to speak of their friend the bitch."

"Should we maybe keep Nils too?" Sivard wondered.

"Um-m-m . . . no. Show the bastards we're in earnest. Cry over the waters that Cod-Ingeborg can look for worse than hanging if they plague us further." Ranild licked and lifted a finger. "I feel a breath of wind," he said. "We can belike start off about dawn, when Nils is finished with the yardarm." He drew his shortsword and shook it at the moving ring of dolphins. "Do you hear? Skulk back into your sea-caves, soulless things! A Christian man is bound for home!"

The night wore on. The dolphins did nothing more than patrol around the ship. At last Ranild decided they could do no more, that the halflings had sent them in the hollow hope they might learn something, or in hollower spite.

The breeze freshened. Waves grew choppy and smote louder against the hull, which rocked. Across the wan stars, inexplicable, passed a flight of black swans.

Those stars faded out at the early summer dawn. Eastward the sky turned white; westward it remained silver-blue, bearing a ghostly moon. The crests of waves ran molten with light; their troughs were purple and black; the sea overall shimmered and sparkled in a green like the green of glaciers. It whooshed and cast spray. Wind whittered through the shrouds.

Up the ladder from the hold, men prodded Nils at pike point. His hands were tied behind him, which made the climbing hard. Twice he fell, to their blustery mirth. His garments were foul and bloodstained, but his blowing hair and downy beard caught the shiningness of the still unseen sun. He braced legs wide against the roll of the ship and drank deep of the wet wild air.

122

Torben and Palle kept watch at the bulwarks, Sivard aloft. Lave and Tyge guarded the prisoner. Ingeborg stood aside, her face blank, her eyes smoldering. Nils looked squarely at Ranild, who bore in his hands the noose of a rope that passed over the yardarm. "Since we have no priest," the boy asked, "will you let me say one more Our Father?"

"Why?" the skipper drawled.

Ingeborg trod near. "Maybe I can shrive you," she said.

"Hey?" Ranild was startled. After a moment, he and his men grinned. "Indeed, indeed!"

He waved Lave and Tyge back, and himself withdrew toward the bows. Nils stood hurt and astounded. "Go on," Ranild called through the wind and wave-rush. "Let's see a good show. You'll live as long as you can play-act it, Nils."

"No!" the boy shouted. "Ingeborg, how could you?"

She caught him by the forelock, drew his face down to hers in spite of his withstanding, and whispered. They saw him grow taut, they saw how he kindled. "What'd you say?" Ranild demanded.

"Keep *me* alive and I might tell you," Ingeborg answered merrily. She and Nils mocked the last rites as best they were able, while the sailors yelped laughter.

"*Pax vobiscum,*" she said finally, who had known clerics. "*Dominus vobiscum.*" She signed the kneeling youth. It gave her a chance to murmur to him: "God forgive us this, and forgive me that He is not the lord on whom I called. Nils, if we never see each other beyond today, fare you well."

"And you, Ingeborg." He rose to his feet. "I am ready," he said.

Ranild, puzzled, more than a bit uneasy, came toward him carrying the noose.

And suddenly Ingeborg shrieked. "*Ya-a-a-a-ah!*" Her nails raked at Lave's eyes. He lurched. "What the devil?" he choked. Ingeborg clung to him, clawing, biting, yelling. Tyge dashed to help. Nils lowered his head, charged, and butted Ranild in the stomach. The skipper went down on his arse. Nils kicked him in

123

the ribs. Torben and Palle sprang from the bulwarks to grab the boy. Sivard gaped from above.

The dolphins had been swimming in their ring for so many hours in order that the crew might come to think no trouble was to be looked for from the water, and stop paying close heed. Too late, the man in the crow's nest cried warning.

Out from under the poopdeck burst Eyjan. Her knife flared in her hand.

Up from the sea came Tauno. He had emptied his lungs while he clung to the barnacled hull, hidden by the forecastle bulge. Now a dolphin rose beneath him. With fingers and toes, Tauno gripped the backfin, and the leap carried him halfway from water to rail. He caught that rail and vaulted inboard.

Palle started to turn around. The merman's son caught the pikeshaft left-handed; his right hand slid dagger into Palle, who fell on the deck screaming and pumping blood like any slaughtered hog. Tauno rammed the butt of the pike into Torben's midriff. The sailor staggered back.

Tauno slashed the rope on Nils' wrists. He drew the second of the knives he carried. "Here," he said. "This was Kennin's." Nils uttered a single yell of thanks, and bounded after Torben.

Lave was having trouble yet with Ingeborg. Eyjan came from behind and drove her own blade in at the base of the skull. Before she could free the iron, Tyge jabbed his pike at her. With scornful ease, she ducked the thrust, got in beneath his guard and to him. What happened next does not bear telling. The merfolk did not make war, but they knew how to take an enemy apart.

At the masthead Sivard befouled himself and wailed for mercy.

Stunned though Torben was, Nils failed to dispatch him at once, making several passes before he could sink knife in belly; and then Torben did not die, he threshed bleeding and howling until Eyjan got around to cutting his throat; and Nils was sick. Meanwhile Ranild had regained his feet. His sword flew free; the cold light ran along it. He and Tauno moved about, searching for an opening.

"Whatever you do," Tauno said to him, "you are a dead man."

"If I die in the flesh," Ranild gibed, "I will live without end while you are naught but dung."

Tauno stopped and raked fingers through his hair. "I do not understand why that should be so," he said. "Maybe your kind has more need of eternity."

Ranild thought he saw a chance. He rushed in. Thus he took Tauno's lure. He stabbed. The halfling was not there, had simply swayed aside from the point. Tauno chopped down on Ranild's wrist with the edge of his left hand. The sword clattered loose. Tauno's right hand struck home the knife. Ranild fell to the deck. The sun rose and all blood shone an impossibly bright red.

Ranild's wound was not mortal. He stared at Tauno above him and gasped, "Let me . . . confess to God . . . let me escape Hell."

"Why should I?" Tauno said. "I have no soul." He lifted the feebly struggling body and threw it overboard for the dogfish. Eyjan swarmed up the ratlines to make an end of Sivard's noise.

9

SUMMER passed, fall came back. The ling bloomed purple, the rowan flared, the aspen trembled in gold. Down from the hunter's moon drifted a lonesome wander-song of geese. In the mornings breath smoked and puddles crunched underfoot.

From Jutland fared a ship: across the Kattegat, through the Sound that swarmed with silvery herring and the boats that took them, on into the Baltic and thus to Bornholm. She docked at Sandvig on the north end, where the island rises in cliffs to the stronghold called Hammer House, and the crew got shore leave. The owners hired horses and rode to a certain unpeopled cove.

Gray whitecaps blew in, beneath a pale, whistling sky. When they withdrew, the rattle of pebbles sounded like a huge quern.

Gulls flew about, mewing. On the sands were strewn brown tangles of kelp, that smelt of the deeps and had small bladders which popped when trodden on. Beyond those dunes and harsh grass was a moor, wide heathery reaches and a bauta stone raised by folk long forgotten.

The merman's children waded ashore to greet their guests. They were unclad, save for belts that held obsidian knives and the water that streamed off their skins; they gripped harpoons made of bone and driftwood; Tauno's wet locks hung greenish-gold, Eyjan's bronze-red with the same faint seaweed undertint.

Richly garbed, Nils Jonsen and Ingeborg Hjalmarsdatter hugged those two. "What ages it has been!" Ingeborg said in a shaken voice. "What weary ages!"

"As long for us, waiting here to get word," Tauno answered. They saw his calm was the thinnest of masks. "Well?" he snapped. "Give us your news."

"It's good," Ingeborg said. "The task wasn't easy—best I not think of how near we came the hangman when the Junkers sniffed gold—but we did your wish. Margrete lives free, adopted into her mother's family." She fleered. "Loving they were toward the dear orphan kin-child, after we showed them a bag or two from the kraken's hoard! Have no fears, though. We saw to it and we'll keep seeing to it that most of the wealth goes into her dowry."

Eyjan kissed Nils as wildly as the wind-blown Baltic kissed Bornholm. "I can never thank you enough," she said.

"Thank not me," he told her awkwardly. "Ingeborg knew the ins and outs. I was no more than a bodyguard."

"Without your skill," Eyjan said, "I doubt the rest of us could have brought the *Herning* to harbor."

Tauno dropped his spear and caught Ingeborg by the hands. She had not erenow heard him afraid: "Besides having money, how does our sister?"

"Very well," she hastened to make him sure. "We had many talks with her." Eyes dropped. "She . . . she is not ungrateful . . .

126

still, more pious than most. Do you understand? She's happy, but best you not seek her yourselves."

Tauno nodded. "I thought so. That pain is already leached out of us. We have done what we could for Yria; henceforward let her be Margrete.

"What do you and Nils intend?"

"M-m, he's been seeing men of the Hansa, with the thought of buying into ships that sail under their ward. Myself—I suppose a woman outside a convent had better be wedded—"

"To Nils?" asked Tauno gladly.

"He is too young, he is too good." Her glance swung to the lad and Eyjan, who were likewise holding hands and smiling at one another. "I'll find my road. Have no worries over me, Tauno. But you?"

"We lingered only to hear from you twain." Eagerness pulsed through him. "Now we can be off, to seek our father and our folk."

The brown eyes rose to his merman countenance. "Then farewell forever?" she said low. Nils and Eyjan were kissing again.

"Yes." Tauno's gravity flew away in a laugh. "Yet this night we can spend in the hut—warm, firelit—that we raised on the far side of yonder headland just for your coming. Glad memories make welcome freight."

He and his sister walked behind, so that their bodies might shield the humans from the wind that streaked in off the sea.

As for myself, I was born in St. Petersburg, Florida, in 1930; served with the Infantry in Korea during that particular fracas; and moved to New York after my discharge, to attend various writing courses and workshops at Columbia University. My beautiful wife Noël and I now live on Long Island in a big old Greek Revival house filled to the scuppers with books and dogs and antiquities.

My first book was published in 1965. Since reissued in revised form, it is thus still in print under the new title of *Thongor and the Wizard of Lemuria*. There have been thirty-two books since then, mostly novels of Sword & Sorcery; but not all, for I have also published science fiction, short story collections, anthologies, and a book-length work of literary criticism called *Tolkien: A Look Behind "The Lord of the Rings."*

Six of those thirty-two books have been volumes of the adventures of a barbarian warrior hero known as Thongor the Mighty. Thongor's world of the Lost Continent of Lemuria is not terribly different from the savage, splendid world of Howard's Conan, although it contains traces of the Barsoom invented by Edgar Rice Burroughs; neither is Thongor himself essentially different from a sort of blending of Conan and King Kull (another of Howard's characters) with elements of Burroughs' John Carter of Mars.

This sort of thing is very easy to write, and fun to write, too, and —since Thongor has won the interest of a particularly vocal and enthusiastic readership—I am content to continue adding a new volume to the Saga yearly, at least for the foreseeable future.

However, as I also collaborate with my fellow-S.A.G.A.man L.

129

Sprague de Camp on pure Howardian pastiches, new Conan stories designed to fill the holes between those yarns Howard published during his short life—and, since I have also collaborated (posthumously, of course) with Howard himself on a volume called *King Kull*—I am of the opinion that I am being typed by my fellow professionals and my readers as well, as merely an author of Howardian swashbucklers.

No author enjoys being typed as the writer of only one particular kind of story. Hence, in recent years, I have turned away from the pleasurable concocting of "mainstream" Sword & Sorcery towards a more personal and original and Carterian style. Towards this end I have embarked on what I call my "Zarkandu Trilogy" with a novel titled *Lost World of Time;* on a "Gondwane Trilogy" with a novel called *The Giant of World's End;* and on an Atlantis Trilogy with a book named *The Black Star*. However good or bad or indifferent these novels may be, at least they represent a new departure from my familiar style of Howard-*cum*-Burroughs Sword & Sorcery.

ANOTHER new direction is a rather long and prolix and probably fairly shapeless novel which will eventually appear under the title of *Amalric*.

This book will relate at length the wanderings and adventures of a new character, Amalric the man god of Thoorana, and his sidekick, a scrawny, peevish, soft-hearted, and bad-tempered little magician named Ubonidus.

Amalric is an Immortal, a superman employed by the Gods of his world, the planet Thoorana which revolves about the star Kylix in the constellation of the Unicorn, to go about the world destroying monsters, disthroning tyrants, and disposing of other undesirable supernatural adversaries. Rather the same as the career of the Greek hero, Hercules, whose Twelve Labors were dictated by the Olympian pantheon and which eventually earned him a place among the Gods.

This is, as it happens, the first of Amalric's adventures in print, and also the first story of the series. I hope it meets with your approval!

130

The Higher
Heresies of Oolimar

by LIN CARTER

PROLOGUE

Zao, Olymbris, Thoorana, Zephrondus, and great Gulzund—these five worlds circle the star Kylix in the Unicorn.

It is of Thoorana I would speak.

No man of our world hath walked her golden fields nor trod her goblin-haunted hills.

But I have voyaged thither in my dreams, and from that far voyaging I bring back to you this tale . . .

1. The Speaking Stone of Telasterion

IN THE LAND of Ablamarion riseth a great mountain near the shining shores of the Cyrenarian Sea.

From the peak of that mountain, which men call Telasterion, you can see the seacoast towns of Dazenderath and Hilarna to the north, that stand to either side of the mouth of the holy river, and the blue-green sea beyond, and the isles therein, such as Yaqqualome and spicy Komyra, and the Gankoys.

The holy river, Uth Chanderzool, winds south to curve about the base of Telasterion where the walled city of Chan Chan nestles against her marble flanks; from thence it wanders southlier past the Seven Cities to wash the piers of Oolimar where the Prophet Priests reign. Eastwards the land grows barren beyond the hills of Fasht and the great marshes and the wastes of Yend that lie in the shadow of the Mountains of the Black Trolls, beyond which is Mystery.

And west-away the Red Forests stretch, and the twisted silver ribbon that is Neethra the Forest River may be seen from the mountain crest, and the woods beyond, that darken to shadowy purple as they run to the world's far edge.

All of this, I say, could you see were you to climb to the utmost peak of Telasterion. But this is one of the Seven Hundred Mountains the Eternal Gods who rule the Unicorn Stars have reserved unto themselves. Hence no man hath climbed it in all the ages since the Gods fell from power and the Faith died among men.

Save one only.

It took him seven hours to scale the great north face of Telasterion and three times he halted, and clung to the wall while mighty winds plucked at him with impalpable fingers, thinking he could go no further for all his massive strength, and three times the Gods lent him courage and he went on.

At last, towards the mid-day hour when Kylix the sun star ascends to the zenith of the sky, he achieved the mountain's crown. He dragged himself over the lip of the ledge and lay for a time, breathing deeply, feeling the swift cold wind on his face and tasting the salt tang blown thither from the foaming waves of the Cyrenarian Sea.

After a time he rose to his feet and stood before the Sphere.

It was half the height of mortal man, a great clouded ball of smoky crystal, and it stood upon a broad pillar of lead.

He looked upon the Sphere. He had come four thousand leagues across the world to gaze upon it, and he felt a great surge of inward joy.

Once, in the high golden days now long gone by, seven hundred such globes of crystal had adorned the crests of mighty mountains

across the face of Thoorana, and through the Spheres the voices
of the Gods had spoken unto their priests, and those priests had
handed down to the kingdoms of men the decrees and the laws and
the revelations of the Eternal Gods.

But then had come out of the Ultimate North, from unknown
lands across the Cyrenarian Sea, the Sea Horde of the Islak Kirioth,
and had laid waste to the cities and slaughtered the priests and
broken down the temples, and the Faith died among men. For men
saw that even the Eternal Gods could not protect them from the
ravaging of war, and they turned from their Gods and created new
divinities from their own imaginings.

And when men cease to worship Gods, those Gods dwindle and
fade and weaken, although they do not wholly die. Thus it was with
the Gods of Thoorana. And thus, one by one, over the years and
the centuries, the Speaking Stones atop the seven hundred mountains fell silent and crumbled.

But here atop Telasterion a Stone yet stood. Had it, too, grown
silent over the years?

THE man who had climbed to the peak of Telasterion stood quietly
before the Stone, and these thoughts passed through his mind as
he stood and waited.

He was a mightier man than you or I have ever seen: our world
hath none such as he, save perchance in the elder days when there
were heroes who went about the earth doing the business of the
Gods.

He stood seven feet tall and he was a mighty man of war, with
shoulders that seemed carven out of stone and great arms as thick
around as the thighs of lesser men. His body was magnificent,
golden bronze, and thewed like a gladiator, with long sinewy legs
and a taut slim waist and a broad chest.

His skin was tanned to the hue of dark bronze and his thick
tousled mane of hair was the color of sun-bleached straw. His face
was bold and strong-boned, with a powerful jaw, clean-shaven,
and eyes of cold clear grey.

133

There was laughter in his grey eyes, a bold joyous laughter, clean and boisterous and hearty. His voice, when he spoke, was deep and thunderous, and it too had laughter in it.

He wore a short tunic of tanned leather sewn all over with rings of bronze. His feet were shod in leathern boots that rose to his knees and were folded over at the tops. He had a great cloak of wine-colored wool, but he had removed it during his climb so that his arms might not be encumbered, and it was folded across his shoulders where a broad strap of black leather held his only weapon, which was a long staff of hard bronze.

He was a man, but not a mortal.

He was immortal, but not a god.

And his name was Amalric.

AFTER a time, he spoke to the Sphere.

"I am here, Lords," he said in his deep, deep voice.

Have you fulfilled our commandment? asked a Voice from the Speaking Stone. It was thin and cold and clear, and Amalric the man god was never sure whether it spoke in very truth—that is, aloud, as men speak to men—or whether it was a voice that spoke only within his mind.

"Aye, Lords," he rumbled. "The Ghost Knights ride no more in Iom Tharma beside the Selymbrian Hills. The reign of Erython the White Enchanter hath ended, and his staff is broken, and he dwells no longer in the Tower of the Dragon. And the people of that land hearken no more after his words, and praise the name of the Gods."

He fell silent. He was a simple man of few words. And he knew that his Masters little liked converse. Their power was shrunken and faded with age, and it demanded much of them to sustain the linkage between Segastirion the world of the Gods and Thoorana the world of men—the linkage of the Speaking Stone. So he did not tell them of the curious doom that befell King Adrastus, nor how the bandits of Kastador Forest no longer fed their victims to the Dweller in the Pool, nor the strange secret Bazdeera the witch of

134

Naozoon had taught him in exchange for her shadow which he had stolen in a black mirror.

These things were, after all, of no importance.

At length the Voice whispered again to him out of the shadowy depths of the mighty crystal.

Hearken, O Amalric, for this is our commandment which we next set upon thee!

"I listen and obey, Lords," he said.

Far to the south there is a city terrible to our sight, an abomination that soils the very face of golden Thoorana. Long have we watched it grow and long have we seen its peoples turn to dark and fearful lore. We speak of the city Yuthontis that riseth beyond the Mountains of the Halfmen.

"Yuthontis," he repeated. "Yuthontis . . . I have not heard tell of it before. But it has been twelve thousand years, or more, since I have been south of the River of Fire, and many things may change in so long a time."

The Voice continued as if he had not spoken: serene, cold, whispering, dispassionate.

The Lords of Yuthontis have attained a terrifying civilization. They have conquered death itself. They have molded life into new and terrible forms. They strive with unholy arts to evolve a superior race, and in so doing they have poisoned the very earth of Thoorana, blighted it as with a cosmic contagion.

Amalric stood listening, his brows scowling in deep thought, his great scarred hands clamped about the haft of his mighty bronze staff. A chill of eerie foreboding touched his spine as he listened to the strange things whereof the Voice from the crystal whispered to him.

Their ambition and lust for knowledge has driven them mad. They are mad with pride in their accomplishments, and they strive now to overthrow the very forces of nature wherewith the world is established on the deeps and sustained amidst the void of eternal space. Their lord is a sinister being whose name is Thun. He was the first of their race to achieve conquest over death. His

135

mind was transferred to a perfect body of living metal, so that even by accident he could not perish. He is no fool, Amalric: he is a strong, intelligent, and supremely courageous being. He will prove a gigantic adversary to you, for his own strength and endurance are as superior to your own as are yours to lesser, mortal men.

Amalric spat.

"I am not afraid of any being that lives," he growled, "man, monster or devil! What if he dwells in a body of living metal? You remember three thousand years ago, in the city of the Pteremides beyond the Burning Desert, how I fought against Gongolar the Stone Man? I broke him down, and I will do as much for Prince Thun!"

Be not over-bold, Amalric! the Voice whispered. *For in the city of the death-conquerors you will have to use your wits more frequently than your thews. For thirty thousand years we have sought to raise you to the level of the Gods so that you might found a Divine Dynasty and father a race of Gods to follow us—for even in that remote age, as men measure the ages, we were aware that we were doomed. You have learned much, but still you place too great a measure of reliance upon the strength of your body—and not enough upon your mind, which we have trained to great subtlety, if only you will use it.*

Amalric bowed his shaggy-maned head before this gentle rebuke.

"I will remember," he grumbled.

You look weary, the Voice observed.

"Nay!" He flexed a mighty arm and grinned. "I am stiff; the climb up the mountain has tired me a little. I feel very strong!"

Nonetheless it has been one hundred years since you were last energized, and we perceive small lines about your eyes and at the corners of your mouth. Your flesh is dry and harsh. Step closer to the Sphere.

He walked up to the crystal and felt a faint tingling sensation. A prickling swept over his skin as the Gods studied him.

Yes. Fatigue poisons have accumulated about the radiogens in

136

your body cells, and your arteries are crusted and clotted with cholesterol. You are only functioning at 83% efficiency . . .

"I feel strong as a bull!" he argued. But it did no good.

Embrace the Sphere, the silvery, cold Voice whispered dispassionately. Grumbling under his breath, Amalric shrugged with resignation and stepped forward. He clasped his great arms fully about the Sphere, pressing it to his chest like a woman. And waited.

Lightning blazed! The breath was slammed out of his body. Cold electric fire lanced through his nerves. The pain was sickening—unendurable. He threw back his head and roared like a wounded lion. His bones scraped in their sockets. White hot agony tore at his mighty heart. He gasped for breath, drawing air deep into his lungs with great panting sobs. It was like breathing in pure flame.

Fiery needles lanced at his kidneys, probed deep into his guts, clawed at the great muscles that swelled across his breast and shoulders. He roared and yelled with all his might, but he did not withdraw from contact with the Sphere.

He knew this pain. This baptism of fire. It was this had rendered him immortal long ages ago, when he had accepted his half-divinity in return for service to the Gods. He did not draw away from it; but he did not enjoy it, either.

And then the pain faded away. He clung sobbing, crucified against the cold rough surface of the cloudy crystal. Now a tingling of regrowth spread through his body. Like the silver tears of spring rain. Like the soft kisses of the wind against hot aching flesh. Cool, soothing, healing. A tingling tide of regrowth and regeneration spread through his body. Through every nerve and tissue, every gland and organ, every cell of his body from head to foot. Cumulative poisons were drained from him; calcium deposits crumbled from his joints and were drawn away particle by particle; his lungs were cleansed, diseased areas had been seared away in the bath of electric fire, and now fresh new tissues and cells were stimulated into growth to replace them. He drew in deep breaths, trembling: the pleasure of cell-regeneration was a drunken, tingling ecstasy very near to the orgasmic.

137

Now he felt it coming, that roaring riptide of surging, thrilling, godlike vitality. Vigor and power poured into him, filling him like an empty vessel. He felt a heady, drunken joy . . . pleasure beyond the flesh itself . . . the clear, shining and radiant vigor of the Eternal Gods thundered into his great body and he slipped, staggered, and fell sprawling on the naked rocks at the foot of the crystal sphere.

He lay panting in a dead silence that rang in his ears. He was beaten, battered, exhausted, drained—and *reborn*.

We have re-charged you with the strength and endurance of thirty men, the Voice whispered within his mind. *More power than ever before. And you will need it. You will endure great punishment at the hands of the merciless Lords of Yuthontis. Indeed, it is not fully certain that you will survive it. We perceive three alternate time-paths branching from the main time-track at a point about twelve days in the future. In one of them you die under the torment. In the second, you live but as a maimed and broken slave. In the third you triumph.*

He was too exhausted to answer; he nodded his head and grunted thickly.

You will find the city of Yuthontis amidst a barren plain. It is curiously guarded by invisible things whose nature we cannot clearly make out: whatever they are, they are capable of draining the life-force out of any living creature they encounter. But there is a way through them. Watch for undisturbed dust . . .

The Voice suddenly waned to inaudibility. Then after a pause it returned to full strength again.

We cannot sustain the linkage for more than a few seconds, it said hurriedly. *Listen, Amalric! You will very shortly meet a companion who will join you on your journey. The time-paths reveal he will assist you in a very important way, so do not shun his companionship. The man is unprepossessing . . . and in the very city of your enemies you will make a friend whom you shall save from death. This second companion is very important to you because . . .* and again the Voice died.

138

In a moment it spoke again, but fainter than before.

Power is almost gone. Be careful! Think—use your brain, not your muscles. If you survive, search for a mountain called Marmordinak near the Lake of Drowned Queens. It is one of the seven hundred mountains . . .

And then the Voice of the Gods was silent.

WHEN he was fully rested and recovered from the energizing of the Sphere, Amalric rose to his feet and stretched. He grinned. He felt younger. Lithe, supple strength sang along his tendons and sinews. A boundless energy, a bottomless strength rose up within him. He stretched and laughed joyously, feeling the heady euphoria that was always the after-effect of the process of re-energizing.

He was in the glory of his eternal manhood and in the full vigor of his power. An enemy lay before him at the end of a long journey filled with strange marvels and grim perils. In the end lay either a glorious victory or swift death—either way, there would be adventure and battle and foemen to crush, and the red haze of war-frenzy, the thunder of terrific blows, the song of steel, war's dark and terrible and shining music!

The man god laughed, strapped his staff across his shoulders, and turned his back on the Sphere.

And started down the mountain.

2. The Nine Goblins of Lakhdool

IT was late afternoon on a spring day early in the month called Eglathdrunion, when the small, scrawny magician, Ubonidus of Phence, came riding down the rocky pass through the hills of Fasht.

The shadows of late afternoon were lengthening into the gloom of early evening. Ahead of the old magician, the soaring mass of Mount Telasterion loomed deep-purple in the thickening haze. Above, the skies darkened towards the wine-red of sunset.

He thumped his heels in the fat sides of the golden lizard he was

139

riding so as to speed its flopping, jiggling stride. He did not wish for night to overcome him in these hills.

Ubonidus had encountered the giant lizard some hours earlier, while crossing the stagnant fens of the marsh-country. The scaly brute had come flopping and wriggling from its lair deep under the hairy and squirming roots of a half-sentient mangozilla tree. They had each paused, magician and lizard, to eye the other speculatively. The fat lizard, doubtless, regarded the magician as a walking morsel; the bony and footsore magician saw the lizard as a potential steed. Weary of walking, for he had been on the road for days, Ubonidus cast a Minor Ensorcellment on the ruby-eyed and golden-scaled saurian, taming it to his will. And it had served as his mount ever since, to the relief of his bunions if not exactly to the comfort of his buttocks. I make this qualification in reference to the sharp, jagged crest of the lizard, which ran from its sloping, wedge-shaped brow down the length of its spine. At any rate, the saurian served to help Ubonidus in the conservation of his sandal-leather.

But, alas, the golden lizard was ill-constructed for hill-climbing, and thus had slowed the progress of Ubonidus towards his goal, which was the little town of Chan Chan, nestled amongst the foothills below Telasterion. The magician had hoped to be at the gates of Chan Chan by this late hour, but the slowness of his reptilian steed in negotiating the hills had impeded his journey—which made him distinctly unhappy.

For the hills of Fasht enjoyed a very dubious reputation among the foot-travelers of Thoorana. Indeed, they had quite earned a certain unpleasant notoriety. Especially during the hour of sundown . . .

Luckily, the pass of Lakhdool led over the rough-sided hills, enabling the traveler to cross the barrier with a minimum expenditure of time. But Ubonidus' lizard was tired by now, and hungry and doubtless thirsty as well, from the way its long white forked tongue hung dribbling between sagging jaws. And, pass or no pass, the lizard was not hurrying.

140

Having done what little he could to accelerate the pass of pace of his scaly destrier, the small magician sat back on the folded flying cloak that served him for a saddle, fumbled with bony fingers at the various protective amulets which dangled about his scrawny neck, and mumbled uneasy runic spells, while casting a wary and suspicious eye to either side, probing every clump of shadow with distinct discomfort.

An eerie, shrill and ululating call reverberated through the gloom-shrouded hills.

"Oh Puth, Ponce and Pazodolah! *Can't* you hurry up a little?" Ubonidus moaned as the weird call went echoing and re-echoing among the rocky angles of the Lakhdool Pass. And, as if in reply, the golden lizard increased its flopping stride and it began to look as if they might at least surmount the crest of the pass and be on their way out of the hills before whatever fearsome creature had voiced that terrifying cry appeared.

Such, however, was not the case.

Ahead of them, a long skinny and pallid shape popped up to squat atop a roundish boulder. Ubonidus squinted at it through the gathering gloom and felt his courage sink. His worst fears were realized. For these were goblin-haunted hills, and that was a goblin.

It stood about nine feet tall when its long gaunt limbs were unfolded. Sexless and nude, its bony body was covered with a tough, shiny epidermis that glowed a spectral and slimy white through the gloom. It looked quite man-like, except for the hands and feet, which were gaunt and hideous bird-claws, scaly and tendonous, and the head, which was like nothing else and totally indescribable. Huge bulging saucer-eyes glowed a sickly and luminous yellow through the shadowy dark. The eyes were so large the goblin lacked true binocular vision, and kept turning its head from one side to the other, so as to give the old magician a full perusal by each visual organ. It had no nose, but the lower half of its head was entirely mouth, lipless and wide, a gash that literally stretched from ear to ear.

141

It grinned, revealing the most appalling set of teeth Ubonidus had ever had the misfortune to see. Long, needle-sharp, glistening wet and bright red were those teeth, and observing them, the old magician felt a quiver of nervous anticipation pass over his scrawny frame.

Another head popped up to pour the moon-like scrutiny of its luminous gaze upon him. And a third. And a fourth. The one which squatted atop the boulder threw up its head and gave voice to that shrill ululating cry once again, perchance summoning others of its clan to the feast that awaited them in the pass. Ubonidus sighed wearily.

He was not without certain supernatural protection. But while traversing the Quastrophian Forest early this morning he had run afoul of a famished bull ganthodon and had used seven of the only eight flash balls wherewith he was armed in persuading the ganthodon to retire. And Ubonidus doubted if his single remaining flash ball would prove sufficient to discourage the goblin-horde from attempting to convert him into fodder for their dinner table.

However, he still had a full supply of tanglefoot webs in one of the several pouches that adorned his sash; and thrust into the lacings of one sandal for security was a fresh and unused earthquake seed. He had hoped, however, to retain the tanglefoot webs and the earthquake seed against the perils of the forest he would face tomorrow.

But it seemed obvious that if he did not dissuade the goblins, and swiftly, there would *be* no tomorrow!

With a groan, he slid off the lizard's back and prepared to do battle.

There were now nine goblins between him and the crest of the pass. They stood or squatted on boulders, glowing eyes fixed on him and lipless mouths working hungrily. They passed high-pitched, glibbering comments to each other concerning this meat which stood before them, and from time to time one or another of the clan would burst into the babbling, maniacal laughter that made them so feared.

142

For not only does the bite of a goblin inject a deadly and incurable venom into human veins, but the laughter of the goblins, the hideous, mocking, jeering laughter of the goblins, drives men over the brink of reason into drooling madmen.

Ubonidus withdrew his last remaining flash ball from its place in his sash and weight weighed it in the wrinkled palm of one hand. These small nut-sized spheres were the invention of the famed Phozdaliom, a prominent sorcerer of Jasmyria who had, during the last century, isolated the magical properties of thirteen elements and thus added nine major acquisitions to the *Compendium Magicorum*.

As the goblins sprang at him, white limbs flashing through the dark air, Ubonidus hurled the flash ball against the floor of the pass and uttered a potent and portentous Name.

There was a deafening retort that all but shattered his eardrums. And a sizzling flash of unendurable brilliance, blue-white, eye-searing, intolerable.

The goblins fell squalling and mewling, webbed claw-like hands clamped over their bulging eyes. Needles of brilliant agony tore through their sensitive visual organs. They beat their heads against the rocks in inarticulate and unendurable torment.

But Ubonidus, who had known exactly what to expect, had shielded his own eyes against the painful flash of the explosion. Now, opening them, he could still see where all the goblins were temporarily blinded. Now was his chance to escape. He thumped his heels against the lizard's sides, urging it forward.

But for all his cleverness, the old magician had neglected to protect the lizard against the searing flash and the poor beast was as blinded as the goblins. Tongue lolling, gasping like a steam-whistle, it scrabbled futilely against the cliff-side, unable to see where it was going.

"Oh Puth, Ponce and Pazodolah!" the magician groaned. But there was no hope for it. He must abandon his steed here. The effect of the flash ball would wear off within moments, and if he

143

had any hopes of eluding the grasp of the goblins by flight, he had best be about it.

So he hopped off the blinded lizard and ran off down the pass, sandals flopping and the skirt of his snuff-brown robe flapping about his bony shins. All of his magical supplies were safely ensconced in a wickerwork pannier tied to the lizard's back, but he could not spare the time it would take to untie the knots. He retained one item, a fat black greasy book of spells, which he thrust into his girdle, abandoning all the rest.

And he ran.

BEFORE long he again heard the whooping cries of the goblins behind him, and turning his head to glance back over his shoulder, he descried the white glistening forms of the goblins bounding after him like so many rubber balls.

He came to a halt and turned, flinging a loose handful of tanglefoot webs behind him. Each of these, upon touching the surface of the pass, exploded from a small greenish wad of silky stuff into a mushrooming cloud of streaming tendrils. The tendrils flew from wall to wall, adhering stickily to everything they touched. In an instant, the mouth of the pass was blocked by thick webs of wet green strands.

Three goblins were entangled in the webs. They kicked and struggled and squalled furiously, spitting like cats, but only managed to become more tightly and completely enmeshed in the sticky green stuff.

The six other goblins came flying, howling, at him.

Before Ubonidus could move or think or speak, a deep voice grunted behind him, startlingly close to his ear.

"Step aside," it rumbled.

He jumped and whirled, to see a towering bronze giant stride past him, swinging a terrible bronze staff.

The staff was every inch of nine feet long and a good two inches thick. It must have weighed all of sixty *diols*. But the big man swung it easily. His scarred, capable fists handled it as lightly

144

as if it were a willowwood switch. He swung it against the side of the first goblin's head.

The results were—to say the least—spectacular.

The snarling face of the goblin simply exploded. Flew apart into a seething spray of grease and slime, pulped brains and bone splinters and gobbets of juice and flesh.

Spouting a miniature fountain of vile, watery, stinking fluid, the headless corpse went flying to thump against the further wall of the pass.

The other goblins flashed past them, rebounded from the cliff, and hurtled towards Ubonidus and the strange giant who had so unexpectedly come to his aid.

Again, the half-naked colossus swung that terrible bronze bar. It caught one goblin in mid-air, snapped his spine with an audible crack, splintered his ribcage, and flung him away, loose and flopping like a broken doll. The very end of the bronze rod, in its flight, caught one snarling goblin on the cheek. It tore away half his face, exposing the wet glisten of white skull-bone. One eye stretched out, popped like a punctured soap-bubble, and became a flying splatter of milky luminous slime. Howling, the maimed goblin thumped to the road and sat weeping, pawing at its mangled skull.

At bay, a third goblin stood on agile, clawed feet, facing the giant. Venomous slobber drooled down his bared needle-sharp fangs. Amalric—for of course it was he—flicked the staff around, whipped it in reverse, and shoved it halfway down the goblin's throat with a brutal thrust of driving shoulder-thews. Fangs snapped and splintered. A tongue pulped. The blunt end of the staff tore out through the back of the goblin's neck.

Amalric set his bootheel against the scrawny breast of the goblin and wrenched his staff, suckingly, out of its dead mouth.

The two remaining goblins came flying at him from opposite directions, hissing like steam-kettles, claws spread to slash.

Gripping the staff with both hands, he swung it in a wide circle. The heavy bronze bar whistled as it clove through the shadowy

145

gloom. It caught the first goblin in the gut and belted it against the cliff-wall. It plopped against the sheer rock-face like a thrown fruit, stuck for a moment in a spreading splatter of stinking fluids, then slid slowly down to a crumpled heap.

Almost in the same instant the whirling length of bronze shattered the face of the second and last goblin, and clove it to the spine.

There was a ringing silence while Amalric looked about for more goblins, but there were none, except for the three caught in the tanglefoot webs. They were enmeshed in cocoons of green fibre by now, and they bounced and threshed and spat, for all the world like flies in a spiderweb. Amalric strode over to them and brained each one with a rap from the end of his staff. Then he bent and scrubbed the slime off the great rod by rubbing it in the dirt of the road.

And Ubonidus began to breathe again.

IT was too late to enter the walled town of Chan Chan, for the local *dashpode,* as the administrative magistrates were called in these parts of the country of Ablamarion, commanded the town gates locked against entry by sunset, due to the night-prowling habits of the hill goblins.

So Amalric suggested they purchase accommodations in the long, low, thatch-roofed inn which lay just outside the nearest gate. Still shivering in reaction to their close brush with the dreaded goblins, the old magician made no argument against this, so they proceeded down the road to the inn. Ubonidus would have liked to return to his stranded lizard to secure the magical supplies and instruments stored in the wicker panniers tied to its back, but the tanglefoot webs quite effectively blocked passage and it would be a week or more before they dried up and curled away.

"It is certainly a fortunate happenstance for me, that you chanced by when you did," the magician said in heartfelt tones.

"It was no happenstance, but the will of the Eternal Gods," Amalric rumbled in his deep voice. "They led me to you, having

146

warned me I should soon encounter one of unprepossessing appearance who would companion me on my destined journey to the south, when I march in war against Prince Thun of Yuthontis the City of the Death-Conquerors."

The old magician eyed him his huge companion speculatively. Had he escaped the clutches of the goblin-horde, only to fall into the hands of a maniac? And what was this about "unprepossessing appearance"? True, Ubonidus could no longer quite consider himself a stripling—he had recently passed his two hundred thirtieth year—but he had always fancied himself fairly impressive to the eye. Especially when clothed in his very best robe of dark crimson velvet with the high-standing collar stiff with goldwork, and enthroned in his carven blackwood chair in the great hall of his seven-sided tower of green jade beside the shores of Karakerama the River of Flying Serpents amid the forests of Adhodolin back east.

Indeed, he had always rather prided himself on a grandiloquence of dramatic gesture, a certain resonance of voice, piercing black eyes, and an over-all aspect of severe grandeur and mysterious solemnity—as became an Initiate in the Mysteries of Oromazpus such as himself.

In mere point of fact, this Ubonidus was short, bony, bald, and comical. He had a high, querulous voice, a long-jawed, lugubrious face, sleepy oblique black eyes, and was overly fond of the wine-jug and the pleasures of the table. Withal, let me assure you, he was a perfectly competent magician of the Lesser Conventicle and possessed a sharp-tongued familiar who wore the likeness of a small green bird.

I will say nothing of the scales on his wrists and ankles, which denote mixed blood. His great-grandmother in the paternal line was a full-blooded Serpentwoman from Ivorama.

"Indeed," he remarked in a polite, neutral tone of voice to the rather astonishing words of Amalric. "And when, *ahem,* did you last converse with the, ah, Eternal Gods?"

"Yesterday; at mid-day; atop Telasterion," Amalric grunted.

An unhappy expression settled over the features of Ubonidus, and they exchanged no further words until reaching the inn.

It was a long, low-ceiling room. Small diamond-paned windows peered out on the purple evening. But a huge, noisy crimson fire roared on the broad stone grate and beef sizzled juicily on the spit. Smoke-blackened rafters supported the thatched roof, and strings of bright red and green peppers, yellowed onions, dried hams and withered sagemint blossoms hung from them, adding a spicy and delectable odor to the smell of cooking meat.

A dozen or two men sat and sprawled about on long benches drawn up before the grease-stained tables. They were oafish peasants for the most part, big and red-cheeked and dressed in ill-fitting tunics with cotton leggings strapped to their muscular legs with leathern thongs. But there was a scattering of local farmers among them, lank, bearded men, nodding over a jug of wine, and here and there you could see a minor noble or two and a few gentlemen in colored hose and silken blouse, purple or green or russet cloaks thrown back over their shoulders. As well, a small number of Gankoy Islanders shared the benches with them. These savages, odd-looking with their wooly matted hair dyed startling shades of blue, and their coffee-colored bodies wrapped about in a complicated sort of sarong made up of strips of orange cloth as thick as the palm of your hand, wrapped around and around the body from just under the armpits to just below the loins, were doubtless tasting some of the pleasures of a higher civilization while celebrating the successful trade of their cargos of djinko pods and waterfruit and skashpo fins, which made a delicious soup.

Their entrance into the inn created a pause in the flow of conversation. All eyes were drawn to them and the roomful suspended all business, in order to look the two newcomers up and down with inquisitive and candid eyes.

Ubonidus may be forgiven if he preened himself a little under the flattering battery of scrutinizing eyes. And it is unquestion-

148

ably true that the locals had never seen his like but rarely. To them he was an exotic curiosity, with his yellowish skin and black slanted eyes and bald pate crowned with a small round tasselled cap of black satin, clad in snuff-brown cowled robes with half a hundred wooden and crystal and paste amulets clanking and clattering around his thin neck. Magicians of the Oromazpian Fraternity were seldom encountered in this country of Ablamarion, and he would have occasioned some comment and demanded attention hereabouts.

But most of the attention was given to his companion.

The seven-foot colossus would cause a sensation anywhere. There burned about Amalric an almost tangible aura of vitality and power. Lesser men basked in awe before his terrific presence: it is ever thus when men are brought close to the living Gods. All eyes clung to his mighty frame, his rippling and steely thews, but he was used to being regarded as a celebrity and paid no attention to the astonished silence that fell when he crashed open the oaken door and strode into the inn. Casting off his cloak he cleared room for them before the fire. His deep voice roared for wine and beef and cheese, bringing a puffing inn-keeper on the double, with a loaded platter. Whereupon he fell to with gusto while the scrawny magician sat by his side and ate, for he was also very hungry, although he would much prefer to be free of the company of Amalric. He could, as yet, see no way to pry himself away. The burly young colossus (for he assumed his companion to be only a youth, and would have been quite astonished had he known Amalric was some thirty thousand years old, give or take a millennium or two) seemed to take it for granted they were traveling companions from now on. And, with a wary eye on the bulging shoulders and mighty arms of the young giant, Ubonidus was in no hurry to disabuse the boy of his notions.

"I am bound on my regular five-yearly pilgrimage to the Conclave of Oror Oromazpus on the other side of the Faftolian Forest from here," he confided. "If you are bound in that direction, I shall be happy to have your company . . ."

149

Amalric grinned, drank off a full beaker of strong wine, belched resoundingly, and pushed aside his empty platter.

"Listen to me, old man," he said. "The Eternal Gods command us to venture south of the River of Fire so that we may pull down in ruin the abominations of Yuthontis and fulfill the decrees of Segastirion. Do you understand?"

Ubonidus sighed dispiritedly, but made no response. He was beginning to wish he had taken his chances with the goblins . . .

"Have you ever heard of Amalric the Eternal?" the youth continued.

Ubonidus thought a moment, and then nodded.

"Yes, I believe Valossian has a footnote on him in his *Compendium of the Northern Mythologies*. Supposed to be a mortal warrior chosen by the Gods of the extinct Segastirionish pantheon to battle against the Forces of Evil, and thus immortalized by them. Interesting, although I am a worshipper of Oromazpus, of course —the Lord of Magicians in my own native Shamathian pantheon—"

The bronze giant fixed him with a blazing eye.

"Know, mortal, that I am Amalric the man god, the Servant of the Segastirians!"

"Oh my," groaned Ubonidus. "Have some more wine, my boy."

THEY slept that night in a lean-to behind the central room. The bed was supposedly big enough for three guests at once, but the giant limbs of Amalric took up all the room, and Ubonidus was disinclined to sleep in close proximity to a madman, so he spent a miserable night huddled in a chair before the fire, wrapped in a dirty blanket lent by the inn-keeper.

He had planned to wait till Amalric was sound asleep, which, considering that he had imbibed enough unwatered wine to lay out half a dozen strong men, should not be long. Huddled in the uncomfortable chair, Ubonidus doubted that he would sleep a wink, thus he would be able to steal out of the room and escape the maniac unseen. He would be far afield by the time Amalric woke from his drunken slumbers.

150

But somehow or other, what with the long journey and the exhaustion thus entailed, the next thing Ubonidus knew it was dawn and Amalric was shaking him awake, loudly saying they must be on their way south.

As he splashed cold water in his face and scrubbed himself clean in the cracked wash-bowl, the old magician sourly heard a cheerful, wide-awake and singularly healthy Amalric—none the worse for the gallon of wine he had soaked up the night before—loudly haggling over the price of two riding birds with the inn-keeper's shrill-voiced wife.

Ubonidus groaned and splashed stinging cold water in his face. He had no stomach for breakfast. Although he had slept deeply, he had awakened with a collection of aches and winces that would have soured the disposition of an archangel.

There was no longer any question about it.

He devoutly wished he *had* taken his chances with the goblins!

3. The Curious Hospitality of Oolimar

UBONIDUS found Amalric in the straw-strewn courtyard behind the inn, concluding the bargaining over steeds. The man god tossed a small pouch of trade silver to the grinning inn-keeper, and turned, hand on hips, to survey his purchase with pride.

The scrawny magician groaned when he saw what kind of mount Amalric had purchased for their southward journey. He would have been happy with a placid, slow-moving and comfortable calagar or riding-lizard. He would even have endured without complaint the rattling stride of a xanth, or bird-horse, a sort of large sized ostrich. *But Amalric had bought an hlagocyte!*

His spirits drooped. His courage ebbed. He had never been on one of those things in all his two hundred thirty years, and he didn't wish to break that record now. Or his neck, either!

You may understand something of the magician's feelings, if you could see an hlagocyte. Imagine something very like a honeybee, only swollen to the proportions of a giant elk, and you will have some idea. The specimen tethered to the guard-rail was monstrous, at least fifteen feet long, with a wingspread of about ten yards. It was terrifying.

The head was half as big as the body, a great pear-shaped horny bulb, clad in a glistening carapace a reddish-brown in color. To either side of the head swelled huge twin patches of eye: they seemed glittering masses of twinkling black crystals; actually they were compound-eyes, made up of many thousands of tiny ocelli. A complicated set of toothed mandibles thrust out below the front spur of the head, complete with a long, obscene proboscis which was at the moment whuffling at the hem of Amalric's cloak. Two branched and bulb-tipped antennae grew from the base of the mandibular jaws. These twitched about in a mechanical, jerking way, tasting the air. The top of the thing's head was fronded with long feathery hairs as big around as Ubonidus' thumb.

Behind the head came a narrow stalk of neck, then the abdomen swelled into a monstrous egg-shaped thorax mailed with interlocking plates of darker red-brown. The horny, chitinous armor of the giant hlagocyte had a waxy sheen and exuded a not-unpleasant, sharp, medicinal odor, rather like the clean stench of iodine. The thing had three sets of legs, also thickly covered with long feathery hairs, especially the hind legs, whose tibia and the first joint of the tarsus was very thickly overgrown with coarse, waxy fur.

Folded back against the top surface of the thorax were two pair of stiff membranous wings. They glistened glassily, like thick sheets of mica, and flickered with tints of brown-gold, dark blue and cloudy grey. From where he stood, the old magician could see that the quartz-like sheeted wings were veined with red-purple: the effect was that of a stained-glass window, the colored segments inset with thick lines of lead.

The hlagocyte clacked its mandibles harshly. It was eager to be off.

The monstrous insect-steeds could fly a mile high, and could

152

travel at the astounding velocity of seventy-five miles per hour.

Ubonidus grew faint at the very thought.

BUT there was no hope for it. Amalric was in high spirits and only laughed boisterously at Ubonidus' fears, his dire predictions of imminent disaster, and his desperate attempts to coax and cajole and, finally, plead that the man god abandon his scheme. Amalric pointed out that the flying steeds could cover more ground in an hour than the earthbound calagar or xanth could in half a day: and that was the end of the matter.

Wooden saddles were built just behind the hlagocyte's head, strapped securely to the rear portion of the horny skull and to the jointed short neck. They would ride together, and side by side. The wooden saddles were padded with leather and looked not uncomfortable, actually. With a long-suffering sigh, Ubonidus permitted Amalric and the inn-keeper (who maintained a well-equipped stable against the needs of his patrons) to strap him in. The straps were complicated; one went around the waist and one across the chest under the arms, and these two buckled to fastenings on the high back of the saddle. Two other straps were locked to the seat, and fastened around each thigh. The whole system was remarkably safe.

With Ubonidus secured, Amalric saw to the travel-supplies he had purchased. These were belted to the bottom of the hlagocyte's thorax. He had purchased, against need, dried meat and kangax jelly, and two oiled, wax-sealed drinking bags, one of fresh water, the other of red wine. Plus, of course, a large supply of syrup for the hlagocyte, in case they found themselves far from grazing country. Then he vaulted in the saddle, strapped himself in securely, and took the two guide batons in hand, fitting their leathern thong loops over each wrist so that he would not lose them. And they were ready to go.

The horny carapace of the hlagocyte's head is insensitive, and it has no tender mouth or lips, so the sort of bridle and rein system used to guide a horse, for example, would not fit an hlagocyte.

In place of this, the rider holds two long hardwood batons where-with to guide his mount by tapping it adroitly on one or another of the flat protuberances that rise between and to the back of the huge glittering compound-eyes. Your hlagocyte has been trained to interpret a rap on the central node as the command for "up" and a rap on either of the two other frontal nodes as a command to turn left or right. The quadruple nodes behind the ocelli-patches yield a more sophisticated system of guidance, as "faster," or "slower," "go down," "perch," and so on. By rapping the nodes in various combinations it is possible to communicate a remarkably complex set of instructions to your steed, and the hlagocyte can comprehend such instructions, for it possesses a remarkable intelligence, although it has been fully domesticated and is quite docile and even friendly, in a cold insectoid way, despite the ferocity and horror of its physical appearance.

The flying beast was developed six thousand years earlier by the great sorcerer, Lokoto Xodar, the same mighty intellect which also domesticated the sea-going dinosaur-like iplocodis for maritime uses. This Lokoto Xodar was considered one of the mightiest sorcerers of recent ages, and a real genius with the breeding vats.

However, at the moment, Ubonidus heartily consigned him to the bottom-most and most fiery of the Eleven Scarlet Hells of the Ballisade Mythology.

Amalric gave the up-node a smart rap. The hlagocyte, no longer tethered to the rail, stretched its wings, all four of them, and drummed them noisily against its back. Then they snapped out horizontal to its body, the larger pair at least, which the secondary wings trailed back towards the tip of the thorax in delta-wing fashion. They began to vibrate with a loud thrumming sound that vibrated through the entirety of the hlagocyte's body. Dust rose in choking clouds. Ubonidus sucked in his breath and held it, pinching his eyes shut. His stomach knotted in fearful anticipation of a swooping, back-wrenching takeoff. But nothing whatsoever occurred, except that the drumming sound of the wings accelerated to a dull humming.

154

He opened his eyes to ascertain the delay in their takeoff, and almost fainted. They were four hundred feet in the air, and still ascending!

Amalric laughed, seeing his expression. The man god had flown on hlagocyte-back hundreds of times. He knew there was nothing to fear, but he had forgotten how a novice might feel. Ubonidus had made the usual mistake—out of ignorance—in assuming the giant bee flew with beating wings like some sort of huge bird. Not so: the hlagocyte flies with wings held horizontal, drumming in a vibrant dance that blurs its translucent membranous wings. The body remains virtually motionless and one is hardly aware of height or motion, except for the effect of the wind in your face.

Before long, Ubonidus forgot his fears and began to enjoy the remarkable sensation of flight. He had flown before, of course—he, in fact, carried his flying cloak with him. But the animate aerial garment carried one no higher than the treetops and is good for a gliding flight of half a mile or so before its synthetic muscles tire and its artificial vitality ebbs. He had never experienced anything remotely like *this*.

They flew at the height of half a mile. The air was clear and clean, and there was very little wind except for that created by their forward velocity. The early morning sunlight bathed the land below in brightness; the hills, in their upper works, and the mighty mass of Telasterion, now behind them, were washed in glittering gold and crimson while the lower slopes still were steeped in purple shadow. Mist lay on the meadows, coiling and milky.

The holy river of Uth Chanderzool meandered beneath them, curving about the base of hills, gliding in a slow, broad torrent across level meadows; here foaming and furious, in the tight constraint of narrow shores, roaring through rocky gorges; and there, in level fields, spreading into gliding silver floods.

They followed it through the bright morning air. Walled towns passed beneath their heels: they looked down on spires and turret-tops and low domes of green copper. Cobbled streets twisted through a maze of houses built of whitewashed stone or pink or cream or peach stucco. They glimpsed gardens, courtyards, town squares, crowded and bustling bazaars busy with morning market. The houses looked like toys from this height, and the people were droll small mannikins, animated by a humorous enchanter.

They flew over Abhol with its arbors and fields. Farmers waved at them and small domestic animals fled in panic from their phantom-like drifting shadow.

They passed over Rinar the City of the Thuls an hour later, and saw the red towers carven with monstrous demon-faces, and the spread of mighty walls. They soared above Pazonda where men worship cats and swear by the Name of Silence.

And Eobusht, and Pomfret, and Iogath, and Salianopis, and Daringorn where men praise lion-headed idols of black chyst.

You may wonder why the scrawny magician accompanied Amalric at all, as he neither wished nor wanted to. You will grant that he had small chance of overwhelming the giant youth, whom he considered mad, by sheer force of arms. But he was still a magician, and there were still tanglewebs in his sash and the earthquake seed in the lacings of his sandals, and many spells in his fat black greasy little book.

The reason why he accompanied Amalric, however reluctantly, lay in the meaning of the word *quasid*. It might be translated as *obligation*, or *geas*. By saving him from the assault of the nine goblins, Amalric had automatically placed Ubonidus under *quasid*. That is, Ubonidus was now obligated to fulfill a service required of him by Amalric, and until he had done so he was not, and would not consider himself to be, *aquasid*, or free of obligation. Neither of them really questioned this. It was evident. It was one of the facts of daily living, and upon the *quasid*-custom the society of Thoorana was built. And, in general, it was a very polite society, with complicated social forms and a code of punctillio, special modes of address and a structure of tradition, just like any other society.

Ubonidus was helpless. He lay under a burden of *quasid*. And Amalric demanded of him his companionship to the southlands, his assistance against the dark masters of Yuthontis. Ubonidus went with him, however unwillingly.

By early evening they arrived at Oolimar. The timing was almost perfect. They were ravenous, and so was the hlagocyte, and it was tiring. Oolimar, the sacred city of the Prophet Priests, lay at the very edge of the Drylands, and was an appropriate place to spend the night, before venturing on south over the desert country.

The city was triple walled, and in the main consisted of stone ziggurats or step-pyramids, each set in the center of a large square plaza walled off from adjoining plazas by arcades of stone column-work. It seemed difficult to imagine how the city had room enough to house a very large population, for each single building filled the space of a whole block. But outside the triple walls, sprawling over the dry countryside, they had glimpsed from the air as they circled the city a slovenly huddle of patchwork huts and lean-to hovels, where the lay populace, it seemed, dwelt. The Prophet Priests themselves lived in the ziggurat-temples, or thus they assumed.

They landed in one of the arcade-lined squares. The hlagocyte came to rest on the black and white flagstone tiles and stood motionless, except for a slight rubbing-together of its short front limbs against its mandibular orifice, a sign that the mount required nourishment. Amalric and Ubonidus unstrapped themselves and got out of their twin saddles, happy to stretch their legs after the long flight.

Amalric busily unfastened a syrup sack and hooked its loops over horny nodules on the front of the hlagocyte's face while it sucked and slobbered with writhing proboscis. So employed he did not notice the arrival of the twenty-nine guards until they ringed him and Ubonidus in with bronze hooked spears. Uboni-

157

dus, who had been happily rocking back and forth on his toes, hands clasped behind his back, ogling the looming ziggurats, also did not notice the approach of the guards until a hooked spear prodded him in the right buttock. He yelped, clapped a palm against the injured portion of his anatomy, hastily drew Amalric's attention to their welcoming committee.

The guards were sour-faced, stolid-eyed men of dusky hue, with long jaws and noses and mean little cold eyes. They wore long robes of heavy wool sewn all over with green and scarlet feathers, plume-crested wooden helms carven like the faces of grotesque bird-devils, and tight leather trousers and blouses beneath the feather-robes. They were armed with tooth-edged glass swords and spiked maces, besides the long hooked spears. They looked to be formidable opponents.

They were accompanied by a small, fat, fussy little man in astonishing garments of variegated hues, purple, peach, three shades of crimson, jade-green, puce, licraune and olivette—which last two colors are unique to the Thooranish spectrum and are not found on Earth. His clothing was pucked, fossetted, gathered, pleated, slashed, piped, cossipped, and scalloped, and adorned with bright ceramic buttons, sewn sequins, seed pearls, octagonal small plates of electrum, stiff gold broidery, sashes, fringes, tassels, and all manner of frumpery.

He rattled a heavy roll of parchment, clearing his throat with a small important cough. The parchment was adorned with seals and sigils, wax impressions and bits of gold lace and colored ribbons. It looked very Official. When he had their full attention, he began reading in a high-pitched sing-song voice very rapidly.

"By Command of the Arch-Episcopal Council Against Heretical Fallacies, a Department of the Holy Inquisitorial Bureau for the Purity of the Faith, a Division of the Sacred Escurial of Manners, Morals and Customs, a Branch of the Superior High Congress of Fidelity—"

"I gather we are under arrest?" Amalric rumbled. The little man broke off and bent a severe eye upon the grinning young giant.

158

"Not at all! We extend the Loving and Humble Protection of the Blessed Overspirit to you and your accomplice; quarters have been set aside for your comfort in the Sacred Consistory of the Holy Healers of Error—" he rattled away.

"What crime have we committed?" Ubonidus demanded. The pasty-faced official regarded him coldly.

"Crime? No *crime*—you have fallen into lamentable error, and it is our earnest and loving desire to correct your thinking so that you may rejoice with us in the one-ness of Brotherhood with the Faithful . . ."

Amalric grunted. "Perhaps this thing is a temple or something," he growled, cocking a huge thumb at the ziggurat. "If we have offended by landing here, pray pardon it; we will take our beast to another area, if you will only tell us where it is permissible to land."

The official became terribly upset. He purpled, he sucked in his cheeks, he chewed upon his nether lip.

"No, no, no! You don't understand! You cannot leave, you have committed one of the Higher Heresies! You cannot leave until our tender and brotherly solicitude has healed the awry-ness of your thinking!"

Ubonidus tried again to penetrate the obtusity of language.

"In other words, we are under arrest for committing one of the Higher Heresies of your religion?" he inquired. "May I ask what we have done—in plain, simple language."

The official contorted his features with terrible efforts. At length he said, in a strangled voice:

"You . . . *fly*. Only the Divinities of the Upper Air may trespass on the Holy Celestial Realm." Having thus baldly and obscenely phrased it, he seemed stricken. He paled, he signed himself at breast, lips, and brow with a complicated holy sign. Detaching a small cannister from his girdle he splattered sanctified water over himself and everything within arms-reach.

Plain talk, it would seem, was abhorred in Oolimar.

Ubonidus had not abandoned his attempts to be reasonable. In a sensible, quiet tone, he remarked: "But, sir, we are not even of your religion! I am myself an adherent of the Oromazpian Mystery and my young comrade here worships the Segastirionish Pantheon—"

He had done the worst possible thing. And the results were spectacular. As one man the guards flung away their spears and took to their heels, hands clamped over their ears. They dispersed in all directions, sandals slapping the stone pave.

As for the fussy little official, he clasped his parchment to his heart, turned lead-grey, rolled up his eyes until the bloodshot whites showed, and fainted dead away.

Amalric and Ubonidus exchanged a nonplussed look.

"Well," the man god rumbled, "it seems we are not over-welcome in the sacred city of Oolimar. Perhaps it would be wise to take advantage of this opportunity and fly out of here. We can camp somewhere in the hills tonight, and press on tomorrow."

"I quite agree!" wheezed the little magician, with an anxious look around to see if more, and hardier, guards were forthcoming. "Theological disputations are a favorite hobby of mine, but even the most eloquent and learned disputant finds his abilities wane before the persuasiveness of the thumb-lock, the nose-pincers, and the molten boot. Let us mount and cease encumbering the holy soil of Oolimar with our heretical presence . . ."

"Look. What's that?" Amalric demanded, pointing.

On the crest of the nearer ziggurat a company of plumed persons were unlimbering a curious device. It looked rather like an ordinary catapult, but it was so bedecked and bedizened, covered with devil-masks and goblin-faces, holy symbols and hieratic glyphs that you could not make it out for certain. Two priests were unloading from a sort of cushioned wheelbarrow a large globe of white glass which they tenderly deposited into the cup of the catapult—if catapult it was.

It was.

The curt crackle of windage readings, height, leverage requirements and other catapultish commands came faintly to them on

160

the evening breeze. The plumed persons withdrew and their chief cut the cord with a brief prayer.

Thunk. Clank. Whiiiiiisssssshhhhhh!

The milky globe lanced into the darkening sky, flashing ruby glints where it caught the fires of sunset. It arched against the sky and came whistling down.

It struck the stone pave a dozen yards away and exploded in ringing shards of clear glass. A billowing cloud of white vapor boiled out of the crystalline wreckage and enveloped them. It would seem the glass ball was transparent, not opaque, and its milkiness was derived from the gas trapped within it.

"Don't breathe—hold your breath!" Amalric roared, unlimbering his brazen staff. But it was to no avail. Either both had already drawn a lungful of the white vapor into themselves, or the mysterious gas worked on contact with bare skin. For both felt a spinning vertigo and a rapid dulling of the senses. The white vapor was some narcotic, a sleep-inducing anesthetic of some nature. Ubonidus puzzled briefly to classify it: had not the sorcerer Jathdolindian perfected a slumberous vapor during the wars between Handoll and Gaprice a few generations ago?

He puzzled about it but briefly; then he lay down on the black and white pave and went to sleep.

Amalric endured a bit longer. He heard the cautious shuffle of approaching guards from up-wind. He swung his staff about his head, but suddenly it seemed terribly heavy. He yawned terrifically.

And fell forward into blackness.

4. The Amazing Errors of Quam Gan Chee

THEIR cell was comfortable to the point of luxury. Walls paneled with scented fruitwoods, hung with bizarre *manga*—painted silk scrolls depicting elaborately symbolic paintings—many fat, richly colored cushions scattered about, and a profusion of small low

161

tabourets of polished black wood inlaid with mellow plaques of *danjan* ivory.

And there was plenty of succulent ripe fruit in brass bowls, trays of crisp pastries and small pungent meat-cakes, elaborate, whorled confections filled with creamy jellies, and a variety of heady wines lime-green, purple, fiery red, and lucent white. If this was a prison, Amalric grinned, so be it. He had guested less comfortably in palaces!

Their Praeceptor explained it by analogy. To the Oolimarines, this "prison" was more like a hospital for infected souls, rather than a community gaol. And you do not inflict harsh rigors and unpleasant surroundings on invalids.

This Praeceptor, who performed a dual function in being at once their tutor in the Oolimarine religion and, later, when they came to trial, would also serve as their Advocate, was a long, loose-limbed collection of bones named Llu nam Puk. He was elderly and talkative and enormously pious, although not a bad sort in general. Like all his people, he had a long jaw and a long nose, and lugubrious, watery brown eyes in a pale, spongy-complexioned face. He habitually wore complicated and gorgeous robes, filled with pucks, gathers, pleats and fluttering with gauds and ribbands, much in the manner of the fussy little official who had first arrested them in the ziggurat square.

Llu nam Puk visited them three times a day, for about two hours at a time as well as Amalric and Ubonidus could judge, lacking reference to the sun star—there were no windows in their suite, of course. He would teach them the rudiments of the rather complicated Oolimarine religious system, but so far he was still sketching in the parameters of the One True Unquestioned Faith, as he termed it. This consisted, in the main, of discovering what they believed in as of the moment. And this was done by asking a series of leading questions, whose replies usually sent him into shuddery spasms of loathing horror. The Oolimarine folk considered the beliefs of all other humans to be a concoction of nauseating and repulsive spiritual errors, and could only interpret their persistent adherence to their beliefs, in the face of the Self-Evident Sacred Truths, as deliberate perversity.

The first two or three days, his visits revolved about a list of incredibly heretical super-errors called The Amazing Errors of Quam gan Chee. These were so potent a source of spiritual contagion that Llu nam Puk dared not even read them aloud, but shoved a parchment, whereon the list was hastily scrawled, across the table towards them with shaking fingers which he then thoroughly laved in sanctified water and scrubbed vigorously clean lest any lingering taint of error befoul his immaculate soul.

The interrogation on their opinions as to the Amazing Errors were conducted in an odd fashion. Having given his two chelas time to read the list, he then held up a bony forefinger and intoned, "One?" If they believed in the loathsome and despicable error so numbered they were to pat their foreheads, an uniquely Oolimarine gesture indicating a "yes," or tap the tip of their noses for "no."

This Quam gan Chee, they gathered, was a sort of Super-Arch-Heretic who had sought to foist his detestable, absurd, and demoniacal doctrines on True Believers only a generation ago. As to his end, doubtless dire and gory, Llu nam Puk would say nothing. But a grim frown, a pursing of thin lips, an eloquent nod of the head. From this they deduced the author of the Amazing Errors had come to a terminus so grisly their Praeceptor was too squeamish to describe it.

As for the Amazing Errors, they consisted of a brief and simple set of some eleven propositions or hypotheses regarding the shape of Thoorana (Quam gan Chee thought it was basically a spheroid), its position in the Universe (*i.e.,* central or otherwise?), how it was supported in the abyss of space without falling to the Floor of Infinity, the question of whether Kylix the sun star revolved about it or vice versa, and other topics of similar, and seemingly innocuous, nature. Ubonidus had heard much this sort of thing openly debated in the philosophical schools of his youth, and was faintly amused that the hyper-fanatics of Oolimar should

163

regard these teachings with such sanctimonious horror and detestation. This Quam gan Chee had obviously been a sort of natural philosopher interested in cosmological speculation. It was ironic, but rather tragic for him, that he had been born among so rabid a pack of super-zealots.

As a loyal Shamathian, the old magician of course believed that Thoorana was as flat as a griddlecake and of comparable shape, so he had no compunctions about signifying his disagreement with the first Error. Llu's delight in this denial was so evident that, to be on the safe side, Ubonidus went on to register his stern disbelief in the whole eleven heresies. Llu was tickled pink.

As for Amalric, the man god, being a man god, of course knew the True Nature of the Universe and its forces (which is not what you or I think). However, he was no grim, fanatic doctrinaire: in fact, the childish passion the Oolimarines felt for purity of religion rather amused him. So he went along with Ubonidus in denying the eleven errors. This afforded Llu a very deep sense of relief. He had obviously not been looking forward to the problem of arguing them out of a set of beliefs he dared not even mention aloud.

Thereafter, their sessions of instruction with him delved into the complicated dogmas of the Oolimarine faith itself. It consisted of a weird maze of abstract, symbolic and abstruse theories about everything under the sun, from the Sacred significance of colors to the proper use of the fingers. As for colors, for example, the Oolimarine pontiffs found mauve, fuchsia, apple-green and nacinth abhorrent and tainted with anti-scriptural heresy. These colors were never worn or used in architectural or artistic works, were never referred to or mentioned by name.

As for the fingers, a complicated astrological theory entered into the picture. The forefinger of the left hand, for example, was deemed proper and correct for picking the nose during those hours of the day or night deemed holy to the planet Zao. If you were caught so-using that finger during the wrong hour, you were considered a ninth-grade Blasphemer. And so on. Ubonidus knew he would never get it all straight. And Amalric, hugely amused by the whole thing, didn't even try. In despair, Llu nam Puk left them with an enormous volume of ponderous weight, printed in small type. It was a sort of key or index to, or digest of, the Sacred Scriptures. These scriptures, forebodingly enough, were referred to as *The Ninety-Nine Hundred Scrolls of Revelation*. Ubonidus was relieved to discover they were not required to familiarize themselves with the entire canon: the index alone looked massive enough to occupy their reading time for the next several months.

The index, or digest, proved impenetrable. The Oolimarine theology seemed to be half abstract philosophy and half higher mathematics, and employed a bewildering and cloudy terminology uniquely its own. Every other word seemed to be capitalized, and every term seemed to have half-a-hundred synonyms, and it was almost impossible, on any given page, to figure out what the author was talking about.

After three days of study under the alert eye of Llu nam Puk, Ubonidus still did not know which Gods the Oolimarine people believed in—or even if they believed in any Gods at all. For the scriptures were loaded with references to such fuzzy concepts as "The Sea of Selfhood" and *"Arimpaz,* the True Light," "The Higher Oversoul," *"Uruvan,* Infinite Time," "The Life-Strata," "The Communal All-Spirit," "Transcendent Intelligence," *"Talakhta,* the Unwavering Road," "Astral Awareness," and something called quite cryptically *"Gournouz,* the Revolving Truth-hood." It was impossible to tell whether True Believers regarded these as Personages or simply Concepts. Ubonidus, after a brain-exhausting hour spent plowing through this metaphysical molasses, came up for air with a weary sigh. He began to feel sorry for poor old Quam gan Chee, who had tried to bring a little speculative reason to bear on all this.

Thinking of Quam gan Chee reminded him to ask a chancy and delicate question of Llu nam Puk, their Praeceptor. There was an odd discrepancy between the personal-names of the Oolimarines and the name of their city. *Oolimar* was a perfectly good term in Lower Pergonese; it meant something like "riverhead-town." But the names of the people who dwelt in Oolimar sounded more Partusht than Pergonese. The Ultimate Arch-Pontiff of Revealed Truth, for example, the temporal and spiritual monarch of this domain, was called Thed jemd Vozht; "jemd Vozht" could *only* be Partusht. And Llu's superior, a dour, cold-eyed old haddock who peered in from time to time during the tutorial sessions to glance about suspiciously, give out with a disapproving sniff or two, and duck out again, rejoiced in the purely Partusht name of Ith mak Jorb. He asked Llu about this.

The Praeceptor's replies were evasive, elliptical and reluctant. But, piecing things together, Ubonidus came to the conclusion that what had happened was just this: the original ruler-founders of Oolimar had been Pergonese. They had conquered, seized, or purchased a slave-class made up largely of Partusht peasantry. These had somehow eventually turned the tables, whether by revolution or whatever, Ubonidus never found out, and seized power, thrusting their original rulers into the slave-bonds. Whereupon, puffed up with their triumph, one of them had given out with Revealed Truth and they had founded a religion around him. Naturally, they would prefer a theology of their own invention, to merely continuing in the ancient faith of their detested Pergonese former masters, which was Wahwahism.

IT soon came to light that their as-yet-unspecified crimes consisted of more than merely having the blasphemous temerity to fly about on an hlagocyte.

For example, they were guilty of *demovariance,* a crime uniquely Oolimarine. That is, Ubonidus, with his bony yellow face and slanted black eyes, and the seven-foot blond and grey-eyed colossus, his companion, varied in extreme from the long-jawed, brown-eyed, pale-complexioned Oolimarines. They—naturally—assumed their racial type to consist of the true, sanctified model and archetype for humankind on Thoorana, and deviation from this norm by any surplus inches, difference of eye-tint, etc., was making mock of the Divine, and a third-degree Blasphemy.

166

Nor was that all. While their adherence to alien theosophies was understandable and even forgivable, since they were foreigners, and could easily be corrected by Conversion, they were also deemed guilty of (1) Bastardy, since obviously their parents had not been wed by the Approved Rite, (2) Puerocide, since by not partaking of the Confirmation Ritual at peak of puberty they had automatically "wasted and profaned" their childhood, which was in Oolimarine eyes a period sanctified to religious training, conquest of impure desires, and the imbibment of Holy Diet-approved foods for the nourishment of their childish souls, to say nothing of (3) Demoniac Servitude, since they had devoted a sizable portion of their manhood years in slavery to abovementioned alien theosophies, which were simply devil-worship in the eyes of the Oolimarines.

The index (or digest) devoted lavish space to the rigors by which such errors could be erased; in fact, it could be said to gloat over the various degrees and extents of punishment they would have to endure, even after Conversion. I will mercifully draw the veil of silence over the physical maltreatments deemed suitable to such extensive purifications. But as he totted up the reckoning, Ubonidus felt his stomach grow queasy.

It was at that moment that he determined they must, at all cost, escape from this hellish utopia. For they had been living in a fool's paradise, lapping up the fat of the land, lolling about on perfumed cushions, enjoying many straight-faced jests at old Llu's unwitting expense. Shortly would come the time of ear-clipping, nose-lopping, tongue-slitting, hamstringing and a certain grisly punishment called *eluctidation,* which I will leave mercifully undefined in deference to my readers' peace of mind. He confided these intimations of mortality to his cheerful companion, who grew distinctly less cheerful. They determined to escape.

But how? Both were unobtrusively shackled with fine chains of carbon-impregnated steel to ornamental wrought iron posts in the south end of the room, and the only door to the suite—a massive, steel reinforced slab of hardwood, suitable for service at the portals of a bank vault, was at the north end, well out of reach. Ubonidus itched for his possessions: he lusted for tanglewebs, pepper pollen and that fat earthquake seed, which must be dangerously over-ripe by now, as they were well into the latter half of Eglathdrunion. But, alas, all their belongings—his fat greasy black book and Amalric's mighty brazen staff, their clothing and baggage,— lay at the north end of the room in a cabinet of unbreakable crystal. It was placed there within eyesight not for purposes of taunting or tantalizing, but simply because the Oolimarines had an ungodly dread of spiritual contamination, and evil to them was contained not only in certain anti-scriptural colors, meats, odors, words, ideas, times of day, cosmological concepts, etc., but also resided in physical objects. To the hyper-fastidious Oolimarines, the very possessions of Blasphemers of their degree of vileness were objects hopelessly infected with nameless and loathsome contagion. No one in the city was Pure enough to destroy the things, much less handle them. Nor could they be left behind to soil and infect the very air. So an expendable Pergonese slave was deputed the task of possession-bearer: he had carried the belongings into their cell whereupon they were sealed in unbreakable crystal, and the expendable slave was expended—without needless pain or mess, let me add.

However innocent and unsadistic their captors' motives for locking their belongings out of reach but not out of sight, they were a source of torment to poor Ubonidus. There, in plain view lay all his little packets of ensorcellment. And his little fat greasy black book of spells and enchantments.

In desperation, one dark night, he scratched his forefinger— without worrying if the hour was astrologically propitious to such minor sorcery—spilled a drop of blood on the polished surface of the nearest tabouret, and called his familiar.

There was a small flash of pink light, a piercing whiff of brimstone, and a small green bird appeared atop the tabouret. It hopped over to lick up the man-blood, and then cocked a bright black eye at Ubonidus inquisitively.

168

"What have you gotten yourself into now?" the bird inquired in a hoarse, metallic voice.

"Never you mind," Ubonidus whispered fiercely. "Just you get us out of here. Do you hear me, Roquat?"

He did not very often summon his familiar from whatever ultra-cosmic hades or trans-dimensional limbo the creature inhabited. The fact of the matter is, they did not get along very well. Roquat was inquisitive—*nosy,* according to Ubonidus—and had a malicious sense of humor. But, then, considering the sort of work Ubonidus had made his career—Nature Sorcery it was called—he had little use for a familiar, although it was *de rigeur* to possess one.

Roquat made a rude noise at his old master, and hopped over to peer curiously at the grinning Amalric, turning first one small bright eye and then the other to peruse him with interest. He slid his eyes a trifle out of focus so as to study the odd striations of the big man's Aura. Then he snapped both black eyes tightly shut and opened a third eye—hitherto unsuspected, and located on top of his head. With this organ, which operated on the Astral Plane, he studied Amalric's astral-body counterpart. Completing his scrutiny, he scruffed up his feathers, and made a jerky little bow.

"Hail, Halfgod!" he chirped.

"Hail, small bird," Amalric chuckled. Ubonidus watched the two of them with deep mystification.

Roquat then hopped to the center of the table, and peered about in all directions. You got the impression he was looking through walls, noting the guards, the dungeons, the torture-chambers, the thumb-locks, and all the other delightful elements of the sacred civilization of Oolimar. Completing his extra-dimensional survey, he cocked a pert eye in the direction of his exasperated master, and chirped:

"Well, you've got yourself in another fine mess, haven't you?"

"Enough of your sauce!" snapped Ubonidus. "What can you do to get us out of here?"

"Don't get huffy," the bird advised tartly. "A polite tongue is a happy tongue."

"Roquat, you iniquitous, lice-ridden fowl, I command you to remember our Covenant!"

The bird uttered a rude, and very un-birdlike, snort of derision.

"Covenant! Fat lot you care about that scrap of parchment!" he croaked. "When was the last time you called me up to sup a drop of man-blood? Eh? Do you remember how long ago it was?"

Ubonidus subsided unhappily.

"Well . . ."

"Quite! However . . ."

Ubonidus pounced on the word.

"However? You will help?"

The bird preened itself, not replying, milking the suspense. He dug his beak furiously into the fluff behind his wing, and a small red insect popped out. The parasite, which had two heads and a sulphurous odor, scrabbled about the tabletop and finally vanished in a minute pufflet of pink vapor.

"I will give you a word or two of good advice," Roquat chirped impudently. "One. Call Arangantyr. Two. Affirm the Errors. Goodbye!"

"Roquat! Don't you *dare*—"

But it was too late. The bird was gone. A puff of vapor expanded from the place where he had been a moment before, and to their nostrils was wafted a whiff of brimstone. Ubonidus subsided, fuming but impotent.

"Damned bird! 'Call Arangantyr,' indeed! Who—or what—is Arangantyr?"

Amalric cleared his throat uncomfortably. He looked abashed. He dug one toe into the carpet-nap industriously, avoiding Ubonidus' eye.

"My fault," he grunted. "I never thought. Guess I'm getting used to you doing the thinking for both of us . . . the Eternal Gods warned me to use my own wits . . ."

He threw back his head, suddenly, astonishingly, and boomed out a call that made Ubonidus jump a foot in the air.

"Harro, harro, Arangantyr! Arangantyr, harro, harro!"

170

Across the room, in the cabinet of unbreakable crystal, a ripple of strange light ran the length of Amalric's mighty bronze staff.

The staff quivered like a hunting hound hearing its master's call. It rose into the air off the shelf. It flung itself against the cabinet with terrific force.

The crystal rang like a stricken bell.

And the unbreakable cabinet broke apart in a shower of ringing shards. The sound of the smashing crystal was deafeningly loud in the still night of the ziggurat-temple.

Like an ungainly missile, the bronze staff hurtled the length of the room to slap into Amalric's waiting palm.

Ubonidus stared with goggling eyes. He was dumb with amazement. Amalric forced a grin, still feeling foolish for not having thought of this solution himself. It is demeaning to be indebted to a fat green bird.

"What's the use of being a Halfgod, without an enchanted weapon?" he asked rhetorically. Ubonidus had no reply to this remark, and while he was fumbling with numb wits for one, he heard pelting footsteps in the outer hall. The crash of the breaking cabinet had aroused the local constabulary. They would be here in moments.

"Hurry!" he gasped in an agony of suspense.

Amalric inserted one end of the staff in the ring segment of his tether-chain that was fastened to the wrought iron pillar. Great bands of muscle leaped and crawled on his shoulders as he applied leverage. With a deafening retort the link shattered. Grains of fractured steel tinkled against the walls.

In a trice he had unfettered himself and was bending to perform similar service for Ubonidus.

Then the door crashed open and people were all over the room. There was their Praeceptor, Llu nam Puk, sleepy-faced and yawning, gowned in startling taffeta nightclothes with puffed sleeves and fluttering ribbands. And his superior, the sour and puritanical Ith mak Jorb. And any number of startled guards.

"What is happening here?" snapped Ith mak Jorb.

171

"We . . . ah . . ." Ubonidus fumbled for a reply, while Amalric grimly wrenched and pried at his shackles.

"Are you attempting to *escape,* vile heretic?" the sour-faced theocrat demanded harshly. "If so, abandon the attempt. It is hopeless. Your chains are carbon steel."

Amalric broke into booming laughter and rose to his feet, with Ubonidus' broken chains in his hand.

"Carbon steel? Tush! 'Tis hard, but brittle. I have broken tougher metal. Why, I recall—during my eight hundred fortieth Labor for the Eternal Gods—when I descended to the Netherworld to wrestle Warthoond the Death Demon for the soul of the Princess of Ollulumio—they bound me with chains of perdurable adamant. Now *there* is a tough metal for you!"

A strange thing occurred.

The guards, in the very act of lunging for Amalric, at the mention of these alien mythological figures, winced aside, tripping over their own and their fellows' feet and dropping a clatter of spears in their confusion.

Inspiration struck Ubonidus like a thunderbolt!

Thoughts flew through his mind with incredible speed. The terror the Oolimarines bore towards heresy, even vocal. The second cryptic bit of advice Roquat had flippantly imparted ere his evanishment: "Affirm the Errors." *The Amazing Errors of . . .*

A vast joy welled up within him. The bliss of battle shone in his slant black eyes. He stepped forward to confront the burning gaze of sour old Ith mak Jorb.

"I affirm, firstly, that Thoorana is in basic shape *spheroidal,* rather than bowl-shapen!" he said, crisply in a ringing tone.

Ith mak Jorb turned the color of moldy whey.

Llu nam Puk went *"Gakk!"*

The guards dropped all their weapons, with an enormously loud clatter of ringing metal, and clapped their hands over their ears.

Into the resultant frozen silence, Ubonidus strode forward and said:

"I affirm, secondly, that Thoorana is *not* positioned at the center

172

of the Universe, but is most likely located in a minor segment of the secondmost galactic arm of this spiral system!" he crowed.

Ith mak Jorb sucked in his breath and tottered against the wall by the door, beating feebly at the air with thin hands.

Llu nam Puk collapsed in a jumble of ungainly limbs.

Half the soldiers fainted dead away. The others fled, trampling the Praeceptor and knocking aside his superior in their frantic rush to be far away from such verbal contaminations.

"Come on!" giggled Ubonidus. He and Amalric sprang to the wrecked cabinet, tore off their penitential robes and donned their accustomed garments hastily, snatching up their other baggage and belongings.

In a trice they were out of the room, down the ornate hall, and at the head of a curving flight of marble stairs. Unfortunately, a full phalanx of determined-looking guards were tromping *up* the staircase under full steam to intercept them. Exchanging a mutual grin, Amalric and Ubonidus took their stance at the head of the stairs and declared in unison, loudly:

"I affirm, thirdly, that Thoorana itself revolves about the sun star, Kylix, rather than Kylix revolving about Thoorana!" they chorused, staring straight into the terrified eyes of the oncoming guards.

The guards broke step, panicked, and galloped down the stairs. Many of them tripped and fell, and performed their downward progress on the seat of their pants. Several even tossed aside helm, spear and shield, to spring over the balustrade in wild abandon, hurtling to the floor below, to considerable detriment of their lower extremities.

"I affirm, fourthly, that Thoorana is not borne up on the bowed shoulders of Djad the Super-angel, but probably is sustained amidst the firmament by the centrifugal force created by the speed of its revolutions about Kylix the sun star!" they bellowed after the fleeing host, just for good measure.

11   Their progress out of the ziggurat was not further impeded by

173

the local constabulary, and bands of citizens fled wildly in all directions at the very sight of them.

To their delight, they found the patient hlagocyte still standing where they had left him. The flying steed was, obviously, so rank and stinking of abominable heresy that the priesthood had not dared come near the monster insect.

When they boarded him, which they did with all possible speed, and commanded him to ascend, he wobbled skywards drunkenly. Amalric remembered he had affixed the syrup bag to the beast's proboscis, just before their capture. The syrup bag contained sufficient supplies of the potent, gluey nutriment to satisfy the hlagocyte for a solid month. But the monstrous glutton had gorged himself by devouring the entire supply, bag and all. Shreds of sticky leather still dangled from his mandibles.

The cause for his wavering and uneven flight was now apparent. Amalric burst into a gale of laughter, and, when his first waves of mirth had somewhat spent themselves, he imparted the information to the puzzled magician.

Hlagocytic syrup was a potent and concentrated beverage, meant to be imbibed in small delicate sips.

By sucking up the entire supply, the monster insect had become inebriated.

He had become dead drunk!

It made for a bumpy trip. If you have ever flown astride an hlagocyte who was drunk as a lord, you will know what I mean.

By nightfall they were far from the outskirts of the sacred city of Oolimar, and well over the Drylands of Wadonga.

Ubonidus strove to console himself with the fact that they had escaped, unscathed, from Oolimar. But it did no good. Even now, their long quest to Yuthontis the city of the Death-Conquerors was only beginning. And heaven knew what hazards lay ahead . . .

If only he had taken his chances with the goblins!

They flew on in darkness, but somewhere ahead lay dawn, and a bizarre sequence of new adventures.

174

A Last Word:

If you enjoyed the stories in this book, then you should also find its companion volume, *Flashing Swords! #2,* to your taste.

Therein you will find a new Pusadian tale by L. Sprague de Camp, an adventure of Brak the Barbarian by John Jakes, a novella laid in "Witch World" from the hand of Andre Norton, and a splendid new story about Elric of Melnibone by England's Michael Moorcock.

None of these stories have ever been published before; each of them was written especially for *Flashing Swords!;* and—needless to say—they are gloriously exciting and colorful adventure stories of wizards and warriors.

Happy Reading!

LIN CARTER